CARTER

The K9 Files, Book 7

Dale Mayer

Books in This Series:

Ethan, Book 1

Pierce, Book 2

Zane, Book 3

Blaze, Book 4

Lucas, Book 5

Parker, Book 6

Carter, Book 7

Weston, Book 8

CARTER: THE K9 FILES, BOOK 7
Dale Mayer
Valley Publishing Ltd.

ISBN-13: 978-1-773362-09-0
Print Edition

About This Book

Welcome to the all new K9 Files series reconnecting readers with the unforgettable men from SEALs of Steel in a new series of action packed, page turning romantic suspense that fans have come to expect from USA TODAY Bestselling author Dale Mayer. Pssst... you'll meet other favorite characters from SEALs of Honor and Heroes for Hire too!

Staying away was harder than he thought ...

Recovering from an accident was hell on anyone, but, for a stubborn guy like Carter, it was worse. No way would he be a burden. So he stayed away from Montana, where his best friend lived ... and his best friend's sister.

Until Geir and Cade ask Carter to check up on a dog delivered to a small town close by, but the dog never arrived. Considering this was one of the missing War Dogs that Titanium Corp was handling, Carter was happy to assist. Maybe even relieved as it gave him a reason to go where he'd been afraid to go before.

Walking into her partner's office to find his dead body on the floor had sent Hailey down a nightmarish path that never seemed to end. Then it *had* started with Carter's arrival. What else should she expect from the man who she'd always loved and who had rejected her time and time again. She'd hoped the attraction to him would have lessened by now, but it was even worse.

As the body count mounts, and the town takes sides, Hailey realizes that Carter was always the one to back her up, even when it meant he could die in this fight that's gone to hell. Particularly when Carter finds the missing K9 dog, and his current owner is on the wrong side of the war …

Only Carter doesn't care, knowing he'd always stand on the side of right, but *maybe*—if he was lucky this time—he wouldn't be standing alone …

Sign up to be notified of all Dale's releases here!

https://smarturl.it/DaleNews

PROLOGUE

CADE SAT ON the steps of Geir's house and wiped the sweat off his face, taking a break from their latest renovation project.

Geir sat beside him. "You okay, man?"

"I am," Cade said. "I'm just thinking about those K9 dogs. And I can't believe what Parker went through. That's just insane." He closed his hand in a fist, then sighed. "We thought the military scenario was the right place to send him too."

"Well, he's out of the service now, and so is his new partner. We'll see a lot more of them too, I think. They're talking about relocating here in New Mexico, although that might depend on Parker's father. Just the two of them are left."

"That would be fine," Cade said. "Parker's a good person."

"Samson too, of course," Geir said. "It's amazing how many of our guys ended up keeping the missing dogs."

"When the dogs saved their lives too, the men developed a sense of gratitude and indebtedness, where they wanted to look after them and to make sure these War Dogs had a decent life forever after."

"So, what the heck are we doing about the next one now?" Geir asked.

"I was thinking about that this morning. Carter Batter-bridge"—Cade pointed at a man who stood with a tool belt around his hips, a two-by-four in his hand, and a pencil behind his ear—"has been pining for his dogs back."

"What do you mean, *pining for his dogs back?*"

"He and his wife had a breeding pair of labs, but they divorced. The wife got to keep the dogs. Apparently though, Carter was really good with them and now misses them a lot."

"But does he care about going after a K9 dog? It's hardly the same thing. Did you know he has a degree in finance? Investments or some such thing."

"No, it sure isn't the same thing as construction. But he's wasted here."

"Carter's hardly wasted here," Geir said. "He's been a huge help."

"He is, but he's also way more capable. He should have his own company."

They studied him and the two prosthetics Carter worked with. He had a badly damaged arm and hand but appeared to have adapted well. He was also missing a foot on the opposite side.

"So, why doesn't he?"

"I think he's been struggling to find himself again."

"When did he get divorced?"

Cade nodded. "That's the root question, isn't it? She walked out when he was in the hospital, waiting on multiple surgeries. Probably about the time she realized he would be missing at least part of one limb."

"Bitch," Geir said.

"Easy to judge but this life isn't for everyone."

"No, we're the blessed ones, aren't we?"

"We are," Cade said. "So Carter here? I think he could do a hell of a lot more in this world."

"But where?"

"His best buddy in Montana has been asking him to come to his ranch for a long time now. It's pretty hard to have a really good friend and yet not spend time with them."

"How good a friend is he?"

"When we were still in the navy, Carter used to take all his military leave to head to that friend's ranch. He always helped out there, but now he feels like he can't quite help because he's not as fit. He doesn't want to be a burden."

"So, what will we do?" Geir asked. "Send him to Montana?"

"Well, that's where one of the dogs is."

Geir looked at him in shock. "Seriously?"

"Seriously. Not exactly sure what happened to the dog—the file's pretty empty. The K9 should have been adopted by a family in Montana, but, when the War Dogs program checked on the adopted family, the family stated they never received the dog. Now the family has moved on and isn't too interested in pursuing the adoption, but the dog's still missing."

"Since when?"

"Three months ago," Cade said. "A bloody long time."

"When did the military find out it was missing?"

"About eight weeks ago when they checked up on him. But again, no time, no money, no man-hours to search for him."

"It'll be almost impossible to find a dog like that now," Geir said. "That's a long time, particularly if he wasn't received on the other end after that long flight. Hell, he could have been lost at any airport across the country.

Although you'd think someone would have found him and called it in."

"Yes, and no," Cade said. "The adoptive family said they had been called about the K9 a couple times but hadn't kept any of the information as to who called. And the family wanted the Defense Department to leave them alone. They were extremely less than forthcoming."

Silence reigned between them.

"Do you think they did something to the dog?" Geir asked. "Like something permanent? Then they didn't know how to cover it up, so they said they never got him?"

Cade slid him a sideways look. "You and I both know people can be the worst sorts. At heart, most are good, but a lot of them? Well, they don't make the grade, do they?"

"But to hurt a War Dog? That would be really shitty."

"Maybe—*maybe*—they didn't get him. Maybe they took one look at him and took off. Maybe they changed their mind and didn't show up to receive him."

"What's this dog's name?"

"Matzuka. It's one of the names I have always remembered," Cade said. "I was trying to find somebody in the Montana area, and I was talking to Carter. He's the one who told me that his best buddy was there, but Carter just wasn't sure what to do with his life now. He wanted to go see him, yet felt like he wasn't ready."

Geir asked, "What kind of funding does he need to start up his own construction business?"

"Enough money to build his first house probably. Maybe fifty thousand dollars to cover costs and a crew? Or maybe not even that much to get started. Possibly a bank loan with revolving credit allowed could work at the beginning."

Geir frowned. "We really need to have some ongoing funding source to help these guys, like seeking out more donations and investors on a routine basis."

"That's a lot of money to come up with though," Cade said, "especially if you consider all the other vets we want to help as well. But then I'm not sure Carter's all that broke. I think he's here because he's lost, like so many of us were. With his education in finance, he could have money stashed away. I think, for Carter, it's more a case of needing another reason to go to Montana, one that overrides his hesitancy based on his physical fitness. Just like the rest of them did."

"Does the best friend have a sister, by any chance?"

Cade looked at him, and his gaze twinkled. "Are you up to more matchmaking?"

"Maybe," Geir said. "We're doing pretty damn good at it so far."

"Well, Carter's best friend does have a sister, but that doesn't mean anything's between them."

"No, but, if they aren't together, they can't become an item, can they?"

"I think there was some talk about the two of them not getting along," Cade said. "It's one of the reasons why I've hesitated. What I don't want is to put him in an uncomfortable situation, where he feels obligated to stay—unlike here, where he can be free and easy with us."

"He's hiding here," Geir said bluntly. "And we all know exactly how that feels." Geir looked at Cade, then over at Carter. "So, do we ask him now? Or …?"

Cade nodded. "I was kind of waiting for the right moment." He watched as Carter took off his tool belt and hitched it onto the back of the pickup. Cade gave a whistle and motioned with his arm.

Carter turned to look at him and nodded.

"Here goes nothing," Cade said. He hopped up. "I'll let you know how it works out."

CHAPTER 1

"WELL, WELL, WELL," Gordon said, staring at Carter Batterbridge, as he stood outside the front entrance for arrivals at the airport. "You're a sight for sore eyes."

The two exchanged man hugs. Carter was self-conscious about his arm but slapped his buddy on the back of his shoulder. "Hey," he said.

"That's it? Just 'hey'? I've been trying to get you to come for … what? Two years now? At least since you got blown up. And, for some dang reason, you walked away from the people closest to you. When you needed us most …"

"The one closest to me," Carter said, his tone a little caustic, "walked away from me first. She left me feeling isolated and wanting to keep it that way."

Gordon looked at him and smiled. "I can understand that. But then your wife was a first-class bitch. I told you that a long time ago."

Carter chuckled. "She was, indeed, and, yes, you did. And I ignored you. We had a lot of good years. But …"

"*But* is correct. Anyway, enough about her. Come on." Gordon looked around for Carter's bags and frowned. "You only have one bag?"

"I travel light these days," Carter said, picking up his bag. He didn't want his friend to think he needed help. He was still touchy on that subject. They walked toward

Gordon's truck, and Carter tossed his bag into the bed, studying his ride. "This a new rig?"

"Yep," Gordon said. "The ranch is doing well."

Carter chuckled. "There are worse things."

"There are a lot of worse things now." He took a deep breath. "Debbie moved out months ago."

Carter stared at his buddy. "Why?" He shook his head. "What the hell? You guys have been close since forever. You've been married for what? Ten years?"

"She thinks I had an affair," Gordon said abruptly.

"Did you?" Carter asked. Carter and Gordon had always had the kind of relationship where they could be upfront and open. He was glad it still came to him naturally, the closeness he felt with his buddy, even after the accident.

Gordon shook his head. "No, I didn't. But I almost did."

"I think there is no *almost* for women," Carter said. "As soon as you think about it, they know all too well that's where your body goes. *Faithful* just doesn't encompass physical actions."

"I know," he said. "I was stupid, and I'm damn sorry, and I want her back, but she's not even talking to me."

"Damn," Carter said morosely. "That's not what I expected. I thought you two would be good forever."

"We would have been," Gordon said, "if I wasn't such a fool."

Carter couldn't say a whole lot about that.

"Anyway, you'll know all that dirt on me as time goes by," Gordon said. "Let's talk about you. What's this about a dog?"

"A job. Unpaid at that," Carter said with a laugh. "It's probably a make-work reason to be here, but I figured it was time."

"Hell, it's past time," Gordon snapped. "I don't know why you wouldn't come here to heal. We wanted to help."

"Because you would have taken care of me, and you would have made it too easy for me to not get back on my feet."

"I wouldn't baby you. I can always use real help around the place."

"I couldn't have helped you much back then," Carter answered. "Do you still have ranch hands?"

"Sure do, more than when you were here last. Business is good, as I said."

"Any of them female?"

Gordon winced. "The new cook, but, yes, she's gone too."

At the look on Gordon's face, Carter sighed. "Probably not fast enough for Debbie, huh?"

"No, not fast enough. But it doesn't matter how many times I say nothing happened—and I was a fool—she still doesn't believe me."

"Yeah, it's one of those hard things to walk back from," Carter said.

"You ever cheat on your wife?" Gordon asked.

"No, but I think she thought my job was cheating enough." Carter studied Gordon's face to see if his buddy understood. When it didn't appear that he did, Carter explained. "She always said the navy was my mistress, and I didn't need a wife."

"Ah. Ain't that a bitch. You always wanted to go into the navy while I just wanted to ride horses. You were after every bloody naval experience you could get your hands on."

"I sure was," Carter said. "I still would be if it didn't

mean riding a desk. That's not for me."

"Not to mention the time you were off on medical discharge, right?"

"Well, the medical was pretty rough. Lots of surgeries followed by lots of rehab. But, yeah, I'm good now."

"Are you?" Gordon asked with a raise of his eyebrow. Carter knew Gordon was asking about more than the surgeries.

"Yeah," he said. "I am. I'm sorry for not coming earlier. It's just that sometimes ..."

"I know. After my dad died, I kind of went AWOL for a while. I walked away from everybody and wouldn't see anyone. I didn't know how to handle it. That's when I crossed the line, as you put it. Took me about a year and a half before I got slowly back to normal."

"Exactly," Carter said. "Life can sometimes send you in a tizzy, and you don't know if you're coming or going."

"Yeah," Gordon said. "Anyway, I have to stop at a couple places and pick up stuff. You know the drill."

"Yep, *never make two trips if you can do it in one.*"

Gordon chuckled. "Exactly. Even on a Sunday. Got to go to the feed store, got to hit the vet's, and God only knows what else." He smiled. "Gotta write it all down or I'll surely forget something on this trip to town."

"At the vet's office, I'll come in and ask about the dog," Carter said. "I know this one's a long shot, but I said I'd check it out."

"What do you mean by *this one*?" Gordon asked curiously.

Carter explained about the military's defunct K9 program and the request from Titanian Corp, the organization he'd been working with.

"Wow, so Uncle Sam really wants to know about this dog?"

"They'd like to know, as long as it doesn't cost them man-hours and money," Carter said in a dry tone. "I'm not getting paid to do this. This is a good-heart mission."

"We all need those," Gordon claimed. "Hell, I had lambs in the house for six weeks this spring because winter hit so bad."

"How many?"

"Twelve," he said in disgust, "and you know we already had one or two other newborns. We always have a calf or two to bottle-feed. But this year the house got pretty darn crowded."

"I bet Debbie didn't complain."

"Nope, she didn't. She was in her element."

"Still no children, huh?"

Gordon shook his head, and his face looked drawn and tired. "Now there's not likely to be any."

"Did you ever get tested?"

"Nah, I didn't bother. Either it will happen or it won't."

"And again that's not necessarily good enough for Debbie," Carter said. "I know she wanted a big family."

"But putting the money into that IVF stuff? Jeez, that's expensive. And not guaranteed."

"But, if you don't get tested, the doctors can't fix what the problem is."

"So Debbie told me," Gordon said in a note of gloom. "Something else I probably screwed up."

At that, Carter laughed. They pulled up at the feed store, hopped out, and wandered around a scene fondly remembered from all the holidays and weekends Carter had spent here with his buddy. They loaded up the supplies they needed as fast as they could; then Gordon and Carter headed down the street to the vet.

While there, Carter talked to a couple women at the front desk about the missing dog. "Matzuka is his name," he said. "He's a huge shepherd and was part of the War Dogs division. He was supposed to have been adopted by a family here, but they said they never got him."

The nurse frowned. "We don't have records of a dog with that name. Who was the family?"

He pulled the notes from his pocket. "Longfellow."

Silence came in an instant.

Was it the right name? The wrong name? He glanced up at them. "Problems?" The nurse and the receptionist remained quiet, so he continued talking. "I am here at the official request of Commander Cross of the US Navy. That dog gave a lot of years of service to this country. He deserves to retire and to enjoy a comfortable life for the remainder of his years."

The nurse finally spoke. "It would be hard to imagine that family would have been given the dog. They're pretty rough on them."

"Rough in what way?"

"We've heard some complaints about their mistreatment of animals."

"Okay, so are we thinking they may have gotten the dog and then hurt him?"

"We're not saying anything," the receptionist said. She glanced at her companion. "We don't *know* anything."

"Do you know where this family lives? Brenda is the contact person, I believe."

"Yeah," the nurse said. She picked up a piece of paper and drew him a map. "Here."

"Any way to contact them other than in person?"

They just shook their heads. "We can't give out personal information."

"Of course." He nodded. "I can get that from the government. Thank you very much."

He turned and walked outside, while studying the map. One of the things he would have to do pretty damn fast was to get a set of wheels. His own wheels. Although Gordon usually had several ranch trucks, Carter wasn't sure how much traveling he would have to do for this mission, and he'd feel better if he paid his own way. Gordon would smack him hard for saying that though. As Carter stood here, waiting for his buddy, Gordon popped out.

"Ready to go?" he asked Carter.

"Yeah, I need to rent a truck. Maybe head there next."

"No need. We have several ranch trucks. You know that."

"I'd feel better with my own wheels." He also knew the chances of Gordon allowing that were slim to none. Gordon confirmed that in his next sentence.

"Like hell," Gordon said cheerfully. "You're just being stubborn. Forget it. Like I said, we have vehicles."

They hopped into the truck and headed toward the ranch. "Any idea who the Longfellow family are?"

"Shysters," Gordon said succinctly. "Not the kind of folks you want to hang around with."

"This dog was supposedly adopted by them. Brenda is the contact person. I didn't bring a paper copy of the file with me. I have a digital copy though."

"In order to have passed whatever checks and balances the government would do to approve them, the Longfellows would have lied," Gordon said. "One or two of them have *almost* legal fronts. And the rest of them? Just a mess."

"Somebody had to have done a background check on them to have been awarded that dog."

"If they were to get the dog, yet they say they haven't, chances are they've already shot it and buried it deep."

"I hope not. I'll be mighty pissed if that's the case."

"And why's that?"

"Because that K9 dog gave a lot of time and effort to this country. The last thing I want to think about is that somebody would take me out and shoot me because they deemed me useless."

"We never got the chance," Gordon said calmly. "You took yourself out of the world all on your own. I would have loved a chance to tell you that I didn't give a damn if have you had one leg or no legs, but you didn't give me that opportunity."

Carter laughed. "Good point." As they drove down the long driveway to the main house, Carter asked the question he'd been holding back on. "How's Hailey these days?"

"She's pretty mad, as usual," Gordon said happily.

"If you wouldn't pick on her so much," Carter said, "she wouldn't always be upset with you."

"But it brings me joy. Besides, that's what brothers are for."

"That's what brothers are for when you're kids. Hardly what brothers are for at your age."

"Thirty-two is not old for me, but she just turned thirty. I'm not letting her forget it."

"Ouch," Carter said. "Unless she's married with two-point-three kids, she won't take that reminder well."

"She doesn't," Gordon said smugly. "And she's not married."

"Oh. I'm sorry for her then. I know it was her main goal. Kind of like Debbie."

"I figure my sister is waiting for you to come back."

"Why the hell would you think that?" Carter asked in astonishment. "All we ever did was fight."

"What's wrong with fighting? I think all these calm and boring relationships are overrated."

"Yeah, but not everybody wants to sit around arguing about everything either."

Gordon grinned, remembering something. "She doesn't know you're coming, by the way."

"That's probably not fair. She doesn't like me." Carter's surprise visit would mess up her days, at least for a week or two.

"She can deal with it," Gordon said. "I told her that I'd get you back here someday anyway," he said. "If you weren't so damn stubborn, I would've had you back here last year."

Carter laughed. "You haven't changed a bit."

"Nope, I haven't. Don't you forget that. How can I possibly?"

They reached the main house and pulled up to the front. Carter remained glued to his seat while staring at the house. "I have a lot of really good memories here," he said. "I'm so sorry about your dad."

"Me too," Gordon answered. "The fact that he died around the same time you had your accident just made it that much harder. You couldn't come to the funeral, and I couldn't come to your side."

"Being at my side wouldn't have helped anybody," Carter said. "I don't blame you, and I wouldn't have wanted you there anyway. I was a mess. I was in pieces, literally and figuratively."

Gordon winced at that. "Come on in. Let's brew some strong coffee. And I've got to tell you how it's damn fine to know you're here." The guys exited the truck.

"You want to unload the truck now?" Carter asked him, leaning on the hood of the truck.

Just then the front door slammed open and out stalked Hailey. Tall with flaming red hair braided down the center of her back, she was dressed in jeans paired with work boots and a plaid shirt. She was the epitome of a cowgirl, but Carter knew she was also an incredibly talented financial analyst who worked in town. She simply lived at the ranch with her brother. Always had. She had planned to build a second house for herself but hadn't gotten that far yet, apparently. At least he assumed so when he saw her here. She glared at Gordon first; then her gaze switched to Carter.

He waited for the moment of recognition to slam into her. Her face went white. However, instead of her saying something he could give a snappy comeback to, her gaze went up one side of him and down the other. Then she spun on her heels and walked back inside.

His heart dropped like a stone. He looked at his buddy. "I told you that I shouldn't have come back here."

"Not only should you have come back," Gordon said, anger threading through his voice, "but you're also very welcome here. Regardless of what she has to say. Or *not* say."

IF GORDON HAD just given her a little bit of warning, Hailey Wallerton would have handled it better. To see Carter like that, after knowing he almost died and had been so broken? She was left speechless. Besides, she had not known if he would ever return. Yet here he was, like her brother had just pulled the greatest magic trick in history— he conjured Carter out of thin air. When she saw him, Hailey didn't know whether to spin away or to throw her arms around Carter and never let go.

She chose the former when she saw no welcome on his face. However, now that she had time to think about it, she realized Carter's face earlier almost showed fear, not hostility. Hailey had seen his injured hand but wasn't sure about which of his legs was really a prosthetic. She recognized his lack of security too, in the sense that he had almost a defensive edge to him, assuming Hailey didn't like what she saw. That was where the tough look had come from. Not from Carter rejecting her. Again.

Hailey wished she could tell Carter how wrong he was. She couldn't blame Carter though. She knew what his wife had done. If Hailey had had a chance to beat that bitch to the ground, she would have done it gladly. This took her back to what she'd just done. It was even worse. She'd rejected him out of hand, and it wasn't for the reason he would think. She groaned and slammed her head against the cupboard. It made a soft *thud*.

"Do that again," her brother said in a harsh tone. "Or let me do it. What the hell was that stunt outside?"

She hit her head for the second time. Then she walked as straight as she could to the stove and made coffee. No way would she give in to her brother's taunting. He spent way too much time taking pleasure in that. Not only that but, ever since Debbie had left, he'd been impossible too. She and Gordon were stupid messes. Finally she had coffee ready. She took in a breath, then turned to look at Carter. "At least you're alive," she said.

"Are you serious? It looked like you would be happier if I was six feet under."

She shook her head. "You surprised me. I'm sorry for the reaction. I hadn't thought you would survive the accident, let alone be healthy enough to come here." She turned and glared at her brother. "And a little warning would have been nice."

Gordon shrugged and said, "You can keep apologizing until you're blue in the face, but what's done is done."

"Next time, maybe, don't try to shock me. You could try being nice and not letting the Debbie issue turn you into a scorpion." Hailey turned and walked out after that.

She headed for the big yard in back, where she could usually be found on her time off. A huge swing used to be here, where she could curl up with a book. She closed her hands into fists. She felt crappy. She had been feeling pretty crappy for a long time since her father's death, reinforced when Debbie left, and *now*, with Carter's appearance, it seemed like her world had gone to shit.

It just wasn't fair. She hadn't expected Carter to come, and, now that he was here, he was more endearing than ever. She wanted to throw her arms around his neck and hold him close. However, the walls that gripped and guarded him loomed even bigger and stronger. They flashed a bright sign that screamed, *Stay away*. But, then again, it had always been there with him, the walls and the clamped-up attitude. His marriage had only made it worse.

Now, however, he was free and single—but he was also more broken than ever. How the hell was she supposed to deal with that? She had always cared about him, but he had never even seen her. She'd always been Gordon's kid sister. This was his first chance to see her in several years, yet look what she had done.

She could feel the tears in the back of her eyes. She wiped them away impatiently. She was too old for that now. She was too old for everything in many ways. She couldn't even begin to explain to her brother that she was thinking about getting pregnant either by IVF or by a stranger in a one-night stand with absolutely no strings. She wanted somebody to cuddle in the morning, but maybe, if she woke up with a child, that would make her feel more fulfilled. She knew it was a particularly selfish reason for having a child, but she didn't care to investigate it further right now. Besides, she had always wanted kids. She and Debbie shared that and more in common.

The problem was, all Hailey had ever wanted was to have a family—with Carter. Yet, time and again, he turned from her, didn't see her, and eventually got married, even while she had been standing right there. Waiting.

Having offered herself once, she wouldn't make that mistake again. She'd been young and stupid, but his rejection had been hard regardless.

It hurt like shit to see him again though. It was obvious he was still hurting inside and out. Was it his injuries or was it that bitch he called his wife? Hailey let out a sound of frustration and kicked at the ground. She knew it would be a long time before Carter would have anything pleasant to say to her. And it was her own damn fault. *Again*.

Life sucked.

CHAPTER 2

HAILEY GOT UP the next morning, made coffee, and ate a quick bite. Realizing she was already late after her crappy night, she headed out to her vehicle. It was a business day, and that was just life. If she could, she would come home early today. However, did she really want to do that? With Carter here? Last night she had finished dinner and disappeared, leaving the men to themselves. She had disgraced herself right off the bat when Carter first arrived. She felt uncomfortable, especially around him, so she aimed for an easy getaway this morning. She took an apple as her lunch, then stepped out on the front porch.

And came face-to-face with Carter.

He looked at her in surprise. "Leaving so early?" Carter asked.

"It's Monday."

"I forget that," he said. "I get the days mixed up."

She relented and answered, "Easy to do if you're not working nine-to-five anymore."

"Life in the military was never nine-to-five," he said with a smile. "But since the accident ... Well, it's easy to let the days roll into themselves."

"What were you doing in New Mexico?"

"Helping out Titanium Corp—the company that sent me here looking for the dog."

She remembered hearing about it and wondered why a company would send him this far away for something like that. "It sounds like they must care a lot about the dog," she said. That couldn't be a bad thing.

"They do," he said. "And, while I was there, I was helping renovate homes for veterans, doing everything from carpentry work to electrical work. You know? The usual handyman stuff."

"In other words, all the same stuff you used to do around here."

"Maybe. I was thinking about setting up a construction company, but I'm not sure it's what I want to do. At least not as my new career."

"Right. Then there's the cash issue. Always handy to have and the worst thing to be without."

He smiled at that. "Are you still okay at your company?"

"Yes," she said as she walked down the steps. "Have a good day."

That was enough conversation for the time being. Carter stared at her as she walked past, and she stared back. Then, she focused on reaching her truck, turning on the engine, leaving without looking back. As she drove, she thought about yesterday, and how today went better. Considering ...

Yesterday she had been shocked to see him and thus wasn't herself. Well, if she were being honest, something about work concerned her too. So she was already out of sorts before his arrival. She believed somebody was embezzling from the company, and she had no clue how to find the culprit. She was in the finance business and handled multiple accounts, along with her two partners. And at least one of those accounts was in question. So, she didn't believe one of her partners was doing something fishy, but that one account was just fishy, and she'd failed to notice it sooner.

Which was even more concerning. She'd been a full partner for over a year now, after serving as a junior partner the three years prior.

Then the other day she had come across some paperwork left in the copier. It had been a double set of books, from the looks of it—as if somebody had already seen the original ledger and was making another one. She fiercely hoped she was wrong, and one of the other partners was already investigating the problem. She loved her job and didn't want anything to go wrong. She had had enough go bad in her life that she didn't need things at work to be screwed up too. Besides, she'd sunk everything she had into this company, her time, her specific finance knowledge, her money. That nest egg had been for her own home on the ranch. But she saw greater potential to invest her money this way.

She couldn't afford to have anything go wrong.

She focused on the road, while mentally calculating her commute time. Twenty minutes still to get to her workplace. She could have moved into town, but she loved the ranch. It was her home, and it offered her a large open space, not like the town itself, where she felt hemmed in. In addition to that, since her father had died, her attachment to the place had grown stronger. Both her mom and dad were buried in a plot on the ranch, along with her grandparents and other ancestors. Hence, the deep-rooted connection she had that felt buried deep into her genetics as well.

When she finally pulled up and parked outside the office building, she was the first to arrive. She was ten minutes early. That was good. She walked inside, disarmed the security system, and started coffee. After it dripped, she picked up her first cup and headed upstairs.

As she walked toward the second-floor partner offices, she stopped when she saw a light under one of the doors. She found it odd since she was the one who had just disarmed the security and had set up today's coffee. Who'd come in so early on a Monday that they'd reset the security? She held an ear to the door in question. She heard nothing. Not even the sound of breathing or rustling papers. She knocked. Nothing still. Maybe someone had left the light on over the weekend. She turned the knob, surprised to find it unlocked, a serious breach in protocol, and pushed open the door. Then her heart froze. She slammed her cup of coffee on the closest edge of the desk and raced to Fred Longfellow's side. It was obviously too late.

She didn't dare breathe, much less move. It felt like everything simply froze while she took in the body's state as it lay crumped on the office floor. A gaping hole existed where the back of Fred's head used to be. The new hole looked like it went through the back of his head. He still held the gun that killed him.

It felt surreal to Hailey. Fred was the nicest man she knew, a partner she respected, and knew he'd never commit suicide. Yet the proof was in front of her. When her brain finally registered that she should do something about the dead body, she pulled out her phone and called Sheriff Raleigh Jones. "You need to come here," she told Raleigh. "Fred's dead. From appearances, he shot himself. But you and I both know that's not who he is … was."

"Don't touch anything. I'm on my way."

She walked back and forth beside the body, picked up her coffee, stepped out of the doorway. She nudged the door more closed, in case anybody else came upstairs. And then she stood guard. She didn't hear any of her employees arrive, even though the workday had begun. Was it because she felt so disconnected from reality? Or because her thoughts kept racing here and there? Her hands couldn't stop shaking.

After a few more moments of waiting, Raleigh arrived. When he reached her, she pointed to the door behind her. He stepped in. From where Hailey stood, she heard him suck in his breath. Then Raleigh bent down and studied the body before looking at her. She stepped inside and kicked the door closed.

"I turned off the security system when I came in," she said. "Then made coffee. I went up the stairs and saw the light under his door, which was unusual because the security was on and no one had made coffee yet. So I opened the door, and this is what I found."

"Did you come straight from the ranch?"

"I did, yes."

"Did you see anybody on your way out?"

"I don't remember any other cars on the road here."

"Did anyone see you leave the ranch?"

"Yes," she said, frowning at his question. "Carter's visiting. I had a conversation with him on the front porch."

"So, he can confirm your story?"

She nodded. "Absolutely. You know how I felt about Fred."

"I know," he said, "but you realize what's wrong with this scene, don't you?"

She studied it again, wondered, then figured out what bothered her. "He's a lefty. And the gun's in his right hand."

"Exactly," he said. "I want you to go to your office, and then I'll make some calls."

"Phil isn't in yet. I need to talk to him first before we tell the rest of the company."

The sheriff frowned and nodded. "I have to call the coroner and get my deputies in here. I want to go over this entire place."

"Then maybe I should go back downstairs and put everybody in the boardroom."

He brightened at that. "Better. Much better. Keep them quarantined but don't tell them anything."

She nodded and hurried downstairs. Three or four employees were in already.

"There's an emergency meeting in the boardroom," she called out. "Everybody, file in, please." She pushed the double doors open, turned on the lights, and waited for those here to join her. Then she walked out of the room. "Please don't leave. I'm waiting for the rest to come in."

Particularly she was waiting for Phil. He was the third partner in the company, and she had no clue where he was. He was an early bird—so, where the hell was he? She had already called him twice on his cell phone, but she got no answer. She left a voicemail on her third call. A terrible feeling resided in her gut as she raced up the stairs, only to be met by a deputy who told her that she couldn't go any farther. In a low voice, she urgently motioned at the third door. "Please check that office. I can't find Phil."

The deputy gave her a horrified look and stepped back. Then, with a gloved hand, he turned the knob. It wouldn't budge. "It's locked," he said when he turned to her.

She nodded. "It should be locked. I wish he would answer my calls though."

"It's probably nothing. Just go downstairs and wait."

She turned around and headed downstairs. It didn't feel right to her. None of this did. But then she had just seen one of the nicest men in the world on the floor with a bullet hole through his mouth. And she and the sheriff both knew it had to be something other than a simple suicide. Fred was a family man. He was so damn proud that his grandniece was graduating this year. No way he would have committed suicide. And then she remembered the forms she found on the copier. She needed to have a private conversation with Raleigh. The trouble was, she didn't think she could afford to involve anybody else.

When she reached the boardroom, she saw one of her employees trying to leave, with others standing in response. She stood with her hands on her hips. "Did you just go against a direct order from a partner?"

Slim gave her an insolent look.

That was the only thing he ever gave her.

"We want to know what's going on," he said. "Surely we have a right to know that."

"You'll know when we're ready to tell you," she said with a sigh.

"But you know something."

"I do. And I also know I'm not telling you. So enough." She motioned at the chairs. "Take a seat."

When nobody budged, she raised her voice. "Take a seat or we'll discuss why you're not taking a seat and perhaps why we're looking at laying people off."

At that, several people sat down.

"I don't understand this attitude," she continued. "Obviously a crisis has happened here—but instead of coming together, I'm seeing aggression and dissonance. What's behind this?"

"We just want to know what's going on," Slim protested.

She eyed him. He slouched in his designer suit against

the wall. His hands were in his pockets, and he studied her with that same insolent smile.

"*Huh.* Maybe *you* are what's behind this." She glanced around. Most of the others were sheep in the pack, whereas Slim would never be anybody's sheep. He was goat all the way. Cantankerous and cranky, following his own way, and just as likely to butt you in the head to climb on top of you. She leaned back against the open doorway.

"Interesting reaction to a company in crisis," she said. She narrowed her gaze and studied her employees. They were as much her employees as they were poor Fred's. And Phil's. *Still no answer from Phil.* She had pocketed her phone after checking for the umpteenth time. She glanced at Candy, Phil's secretary. "Candy, do you know where Phil is?"

Candy looked worried. "I can't remember. If you let me get to my computer, I could tell you. I have a schedule there."

"No, don't worry about it. I'm sure he'll show up."

"The alternative would be interesting," Slim said.

Hailey stiffened and wondered just how far he would go with that attitude. She hadn't wanted to hire him in the first place, but he was related to Fred, and so Fred had asked her to hire him. What if Slim really was involved in this as part of some delusional plan to become one of the company's partners? The thought left Hailey bitter, but she reassured herself that she, Fred, and Phil had closed that loophole. Their rule was, if one of them died, the company would be left to the other two. And now that she thought about it, of course, that gave both her and Phil a prime motive for Fred's murder.

Or gave Slim two more people to kill.

Just as she was thinking about asking the sheriff for more

answers, he called out behind her. "Hailey, come here."

Slim popped his head out, but the sheriff gave him a bland stare. "Is your name *Hailey*?"

"It can be," Slim said with a shrug. "If that's what you want to call me so I can get answers. I have work to do today."

"Nobody will be doing any work here today, other than my people," the sheriff said. He motioned to Hailey, and she stepped forward to whisper to him. A deputy took her place at the doorway to the conference room.

"They're not handling the waiting well."

"Tough," he said. "Do you know where Phil is?"

"No. I've been trying to contact him all day. Or all morning." She nodded toward the others. "Why don't you tell them? They need to stop barking at the door and understand why they're being held."

"Fine, but I can't stand tears." He sighed, then walked into the center of the conference room. Hailey stood by the door and kept her eyes on Slim as Raleigh spoke. Cries of horror rose, and a few sobs echoed. Meanwhile, Slim's face betrayed nothing. Not shock nor disbelief. And definitely not grief. She was sure Slim's only thoughts were about who would take Fred's position.

Then, as if everyone had the same thought—or at least something along the lines of it—they all turned to look at her. She nodded. "Now you know why I couldn't say anything."

The secretaries blubbered together, their arms around each other. Fred had been a well-loved partner. He'd also been the founder.

"Is that why you asked where Phil is?" Candy asked.

"It would be nice to tell him in person," Hailey said.

"Much better than him hearing about it on the news. Of which there is a complete blackout." She gave Slim a pointed look. He was already on his phone. "Anybody who lets out a word about this faces immediate firing."

Slim glared at her.

"And, yes, you in particular, Slim. We're prohibiting social media, phoning, or texting. Hand your phones over to Raleigh, everyone. Failure to do so will have us assume you had something to do with this." Her voice was harsh, strident, and cold. She had zero tolerance for anybody who would take advantage of a man's death like that.

While Slim continued his protest, Raleigh stepped forward and removed the phone from his hand. "Looks like you got your first one to fire. He posted on Facebook."

She glared at Slim. "What account?"

"My personal account," he said in insolence.

"As far as I'm concerned," she turned to Raleigh, "you should take him down for questioning, and we'll post that on the company website along with his termination." Her voice was calm, but she knew what kind of reaction she would get.

Slim straightened. "Hey, look. I didn't post it yet. You can see that I didn't hit Send yet."

"But that's what you were planning on doing, wasn't it? You have no loyalty to either your company or your own family. Fred was a good man. He deserved a hell of a lot better from you."

She took the phone, canceled the post, then gave it back to Raleigh. "Your phone stays here, but you are now terminated."

"You can't do that! I'm related to Fred."

"Well, guess what? He is now gone, and I just fired you.

The door's behind you. Use it." She waited.

He straightened up after a moment and glared at her. "You're not top bitch now," he said.

"I *am* top bitch," she snapped. "And don't you forget it."

"Phil will have something to say about this."

"Phil will have a lot to say about it," she said. "Especially when he finds out you were going to post Fred's death on social media." She looked at the others. "Did anybody else cross that line?" Every head shook. She nodded. "Your accounts will be monitored."

Hailey turned to Slim. "You're under a code of silence. Otherwise there'll be a pending lawsuit." Slim was at a loss for words and did nothing but glare at her instead. She pointed at the door. "I'm the one who said you should be leaving, but I presume Raleigh has a lot of good reasons why you should be separated into your own room to question you."

Raleigh nodded his head once. "But not where he has access to a computer. This is extremely sensitive information." He turned to the other employees. "And obviously it would be nice if some of you would show some restraint and care for the person who gave you your paychecks."

Some of the women shifted from foot to foot. They looked a little uncomfortable, but Slim didn't. They waited for the deputy to search him.

After Slim was removed to a side room, under deputy guard, Raleigh called Hailey over again. "How dangerous is he?"

"In this business? He knows nothing about the finance world yet enough about computers to cause problems with the company and our clients," she said. "He's been a thorn in my side ever since he was hired. Even now, he's calculating how he can take over Fred's spot at the top of the company."

Raleigh winced. "Is that likely?"

"In his head, yes. In actuality, no," she said. "Even though this information will make me one of the two prime suspects, the partners decided a long time ago that, if one of us were to die, the power goes to the remaining two. So, nobody steps into Fred's position, and now Phil and I both have more control over the company."

The sheriff gave a low whistle.

She sighed. "But I can't find Phil. He's not answering his phone. His office up there is locked too." Hailey looked into Raleigh's eyes. "I would like permission to unlock that door and make sure he's not in there in the same state as Fred."

"Do you think that's possible?" Raleigh asked in a low voice, his gaze searching.

"I wouldn't have said Fred's death was possible. Not like that." She rummaged in her pockets and brought out the keys. "Come with me?"

She held her breath as she unlocked the door to Phil's office and didn't dare breathe until after they found no body. "Well, thank heavens for that," she said.

"Are you really thinking something happened to him?"

"I didn't think anything would happen to Fred and look what happened."

"Good point." The sheriff looked around Phil's office. "Does anything look changed or different?"

"That." Hailey motioned to the open window. "Phil is a sweater person and is always cold."

Raleigh sighed. "You're right. He's always chilly." He strode over to poke his head outside and to survey the grounds below. Finding nothing of note, he drew back inside, leaving the window untouched.

"You remember the sweaters he always wore, right?"

The sheriff got a lopsided grin on his face. "And I remember his wife trying to deep-six those sweaters into the garbage and him pulling them back out every damn time."

"Exactly. He never got hot, and he never *ever* had this window open."

"Somebody could climb down from here, to the overhang at the rear door, then jump into the bushes to each side." Raleigh frowned. "We'll dust it for prints."

"Good idea."

"Plus," the sheriff continued, pointing to the window, "where is the parking lot camera in relation to this window?"

"Uh-oh," Hailey said. "This is the backside of the building, with the majority of the parking on the front and the east sides. So this area under the window is not in the camera's range."

The sheriff made a grimace as he tilted his head.

"Maybe you should send a deputy to Phil's house too. I've tried calling his wife, Betty's, phone, but she isn't answering either."

The sheriff's face shut down. "This is looking worse."

"I don't want it to get any worse than it already is." Hailey's voice broke. "Fred was like a father to me."

"I know he was. I'm sorry."

She nodded and focused on breathing properly.

"We'll interview everybody here," Raleigh continued. "Let's start with you."

"Whatever you need." Hailey's body wanted to collapse in on herself. Her soul was already crying for the loss of a good friend. "When we're completely private, I have something else I need to talk to you about as well. It might be related."

The sheriff's gaze narrowed. "Good enough. Let's do a preliminary now, then come to my office later."

She nodded, as he motioned for her to have a seat in her office.

"We'll verify with that Carter person that you were home earlier," Raleigh started. "What about the rest of the staff though? Any problems?"

"*Slim.* He's insolent and thinks he's above doing a day's work. Because he's Fred's grandnephew, he thinks the company owes him."

"Yeah. He's always been that way."

"As long as I have known him, yes. He doesn't like to be chopped down, yet constantly pushes people's buttons so all you feel like doing is hitting him."

"Obviously hard feelings exist between the two of you."

"Especially now that I fired him. He didn't like having a female boss."

Raleigh nodded slowly. "You think he is dangerous in the other sense?"

"Everybody's dangerous in the right situation. I wouldn't have thought so in his case, but I can't be sure."

"Good enough. Why don't you head on home, and I'll call you when I'm done? Then how about I meet you back at my office?"

"Good enough. You know I have a lot of work to do too, right?"

"Got it," Raleigh said, "but not today."

"Can I take my laptop and go home?"

"Yes, but I don't need to tell you that I don't want you to delete any files."

"No, you don't need to tell me that," she said. She stopped and turned to look back at him. "Fred was a good man. He didn't deserve this."

"No, he didn't."

She grabbed her purse and laptop and walked downstairs and left the building. She was the only one free to go, but it didn't feel like freedom. It felt like a life sentence.

CARTER SAT OUTSIDE on the front porch and sipped his morning coffee. Gordon was off doing chores but wouldn't let Carter come with him. So, here he was, watching the breeze go by and trying to figure out what he would do about the missing dog, while waiting on his buddy to join him. And then things got interesting. A plume of dust came toward him, and he frowned as Hailey flew in. The look on her face said she had had some news.

"What happened?" he asked in a voice harsher than he meant.

The story left her in a rush, and the words tumbled against each other. Then, when she was done, she took several gasping breaths. "And you're not to tell anyone."

"I barely knew the man, but that's sad, very sad." Carter hesitated before he spoke again. "Are you sure it wasn't suicide?"

"No, I'm not, but the gun was in his wrong hand. He was a lefty."

"Right," Carter said and winced. "You'd think somebody intent on murdering someone and getting away with it would check that."

"But they might not have been thinking clearly at the

time," she said. "Right now, the rest of the company is sequestered while the sheriff interviews everyone. They're on a publicity ban too. One of my employees was already trying to post the news on Facebook."

He frowned at her.

She nodded. "He was already in trouble over other infractions," she continued, "so I fired him on the spot."

"Ouch." Carter couldn't help but smile. "You really know how to cause trouble, don't you?"

"Not only that but he's the dead man's family."

His smile fell. "Do you think he did it?"

"It would make me happy to think so, but I'm not sure he's *that* kind of dangerous. Though I've been wrong before, so I really don't know."

"Right," Carter said. "Sorry, it sounds like a really crappy morning."

"I have to meet the sheriff at his office as soon as he's done the interviews."

"You're not a suspect, are you?"

"If I'm not, I should be. With one of the partners out of the picture, the other two of us split his shares."

"Wow. Is that normal?"

"We were brought in by Fred, the founding partner, and Fred got our money for our shares. So, in a way, yes, but it also gives us a motive for murder."

"You're the last one who would ever kill anyone to move up in the corporate world. You're too damn stubborn."

At that, she stiffened and slowly turned to look at him. "You're right," she said calmly. "I am. I make my own way, or I don't. It's just that easy." Hailey then turned and headed inside.

Carter swore under his breath. Something about her was

so damn prickly all the time. He never could quite understand it, but the two of them seemed to always argue and to say the wrong thing. He stepped inside, found her in the kitchen at the coffeepot, getting a cup, and apologized. "That was a very insensitive thing to say. I didn't mean to insult you. You've already had a shitty morning."

"Apology accepted but whatever. You and I have been at each other's throats since we first met."

"Why is that?" Carter was genuinely interested in her answer.

However, she only gave a half snort. "You really don't know, do you?"

His frown deepened as he studied her features. "No, I don't. Why?"

She shook her head and dumped the coffee into the kitchen sink, leaving her cup on the ledge, and left the house, probably walking in the direction of the horse barn. All the while, she had pointedly ignored him.

He wondered about her statement, but nothing came to mind. He knew her brother had often said the two of them shot sparks off each other, so Carter figured something about him rubbed her the wrong way. She wasn't attracted to him. She had never revealed herself to be. At least, not since she was much younger, too young to know better. So, he had no clue what was going on between them. He tried being nice, but, more often than not, he ended up just being snappy, like her.

As he continued to consider his relationship with Hailey, a text from Geir came through.

You land okay?

Carter realized he hadn't had any contact with the guys at Titanium Corp since his arrival. He updated Geir with his gathered tidbit of news regarding the missing K9.

Don't like the sound of that info on the dog's adoptive family. came back the response.

Neither do I. I'll check them out today.

Do it quietly. I'd hate to think the dog's been put down.

Chances are, it ran—if it could. Nothing stupid about these dogs. They also have great instincts.

I'll talk to Commander Cross about the adoption process too, Geir texted back. **Sounds like they were having some issues with this family.**

I don't think the issues were found during the application process. Apparently this family has all the bells and whistles to make themselves look good. Inside, though, they're pretty lawless.

Damn. Too many of those are out there as it is. I'd hate to see one of our dogs end up in that type of hellhole.

We can only do what we can do. I'll update you later today. After that, Carter grabbed his keys and his wallet. Just as he was about to head out, however, Hailey stepped into the doorway and glared at him. "Did you eat?"

He shook his head. "I'll stop at a restaurant in town."

She leaned against the door. "Why? Our food not good enough for you?"

He could feel his temper rise. "I don't know what the hell's your problem, and I'm sorry if my being here is once again an irritant, but, if you want me to leave, just say so."

"You know my brother would be incredibly upset."

"He's a big boy and can deal with it, can't he? I'll stay in town and see him whenever he's got some time. We don't have to sit here and snipe at each other. I know you hate my guts, for God only knows what reason."

At that, she stiffened. In a small voice, she said, "I don't hate your guts. I don't have any energy to hate anyone." And just like that, she left him again.

Carter groaned in frustration. Once again, he'd let Hailey goad him into an argument.

Gordon stepped through the door, joining his buddy on the porch. "You just don't get it, do you?"

"What is it that I don't get?" The last thing he needed was his best friend on his case too.

"She's into you in a big way," Gordon answered. "I can't believe you haven't figured that out yet."

"No way. All she does is snipe and argue with me."

"Well, you broke her heart not once but twice. What would you expect?"

Carter froze. "What are you talking about?"

"You remember that incident when she was a teen?"

"Of course I do. It was the sweetest offer I've ever had, but how the hell would I ever take her up on that? She was too young, and she was your sister."

"Rejection number one for a young woman just coming into herself. Rejection number two? You married that bitch." Gordon walked back inside to the kitchen and poured himself a cup of coffee.

Carter cautiously followed, hoping to avoid Hailey until she calmed down again.

"No way in hell are you going into town to grab a meal. Give me ten minutes, and I'll have bacon and eggs on the table."

"I didn't want to be a bother," Carter said.

Gordon shot him a hard look. "You need to get off your high horse. You've never been a bother. Christ, we've known each other since you first came here for the summer during high school. Both your parents were still alive then. That was the first of many summers, and I always knew you'd settle somewhere close by. This has always been your home, exactly the same as it was every time you had some leave coming and came here. I kept hoping you'd come a couple years ago and stay. We wouldn't have all this awkwardness now. I don't consider you any less than you were before. In fact, I consider you a hell of a lot more. I don't think I could have been as brave or could have recovered as fast or as well as you did. Hell, I'm trying to deal with Debbie walking out on me, and I'm going to pieces."

"Yeah, that's because you still love her," Carter said. "I stopped loving my wife once I realized who and what she was. I'm just mad at myself for not having seen it earlier."

"Lust is one of those things that needs time to burn up and then to burn out, so you don't make stupid permanent decisions."

"Isn't that the truth?" Carter grimaced. "When I found out she was leaving me, a nurse overheard and came to me with a joke. She asked me, 'Do you know why men always name their penises?' At that time, I thought she was off her rocker. I told her no and asked her why. Then she smirked as she gave me the answer. 'So the major decisions in life aren't made by a stranger.' Then she walked off, laughing. I couldn't forget her words after that."

Gordon stared at him, then howled. "Oh, my God, that's great. And too damn true."

"Right, and it explains your lack of judgment, but don't make any life decisions based on it. You and Debbie have love. My wife and I were never anywhere near as close as you and Debbie were."

"Then I blew it," Gordon said calmly. "And I've got nobody to blame but myself. That doesn't make me feel any better."

"Maybe, but what are you doing to win her back?"

"I was thinking to give her time," Gordon admitted.

"You may want to rethink that," Carter said. "A dozen men could be sniffing around her heels. She's extremely well respected, beautiful, capable, and the homemaker everybody dreams about having. She's one of the hardest working women I know. And if she wasn't somebody I considered my sister, I'd be going after her myself."

Gordon slammed down the frying pan hard and glared at him.

Carter didn't back down. "I'm serious. She's perfect. I also know she's perfect for you. And, if you're going to be an ass and sit here and give her *time*, chances are you'll give her too much, and she'll find somebody who'll look after her the way she thinks you should have."

"It's not that I wasn't looking after her," he protested.

"No, but you needed to acknowledge the one thing she desired in her life. She wanted children. *Now*. Whether you two decide down the road to not have any children isn't the issue. Not *now*. Whether you choose to adopt if you can't have kids *is* the issue now. Especially if she decides that journey is not what she wants. But you have to at least bring that elephant in the room, shake it out, discuss the pros and cons, plus what you'll do about it. You can't just ignore it."

"I was busy," Gordon muttered.

"No, you were turning a blind eye." Carter was harsh, but his friend needed to know. He watched as Gordon tortured the bacon in the pan. So Carter walked to the fridge, pulled out the eggs, and cracked them into a bowl.

"Did I say I wanted scrambled eggs?" Gordon asked.

"You always eat scrambled eggs," Carter said. "You always eat steak and a baked potato. You always eat white bread too."

"What are you saying?"

"I'm saying you're predictable. I'm saying Debbie would know exactly what you were thinking at any time because you're a man of habits."

"So then why is she upset with me?"

"Because you flirting with another woman is out of the ordinary," Carter said quietly. "And that means that woman's special. Even if you didn't take that step, it's not like you've ever done this before, have you?"

Gordon shook his head.

"So, for Debbie, that set off all the alarms."

Gordon put the cooked bacon on a paper towel to drain off some of the grease and dumped in the eggs. As he stirred, he looked at Carter and said, "I don't understand why I was attracted to this other woman."

"I don't think it's so much that you were attracted to her as you were dealing with problems with Debbie. Your wife wanted something you didn't have to give. Something you're afraid you can't give her."

"I guess I never really thought about it in that way. I expected children to come along naturally. And they haven't."

"It didn't bother you?"

"At the moment, while I'm young? No." He looked around at the ranch hands outside his window. "Down the road, maybe twenty to thirty years, I could be regretting not having children though. I don't know what that would look like. Except lonely."

"Exactly. Particularly if you're all alone," Carter pointed

out.

Within minutes, the two of them were sitting at the table.

As they ate, Carter looked at Gordon and asked, "You didn't offer Hailey any?"

"No. I figured she didn't want anything to do with you right now."

"Which is also why I was planning on staying in town. I have to go in anyway, and it just seems more convenient and less troublesome to have a meal in town."

"Not happening. And you have to watch out for those Longfellows."

"As in, I need to carry a weapon?"

"Oh, no. They're not rednecks or preppers or anything like that. They're definitely slimy and not the kind of people we hang out with, but, when I say *slime*, I mean businesslike slime. They're political slime, and they'll come at you in a three-piece suit with a smile on their faces, then stab you in the back when you aren't looking."

The realization hit Carter. "Which is how they got the K9 adoption application through."

"Exactly. Highly regarded by anybody who doesn't know them, and those who do won't deal with them. But they have money, and they have power, so not everyone has a choice in the matter."

"Are they connected to Hailey's company?"

"Yes, but they are connected to everyone and almost every business in town, so that's nothing unique."

Just then Hailey walked in and went straight to the table to glare at Carter. "Why would you ask that?"

Carter's eyebrows shot up. He studied the woman he had always liked but never managed to get past the prickly stage with. "Because, when there's trouble in town, it rarely comes from multiple sources at once. If you have a trouble spot, and there's something political behind this murder, then you have to look at those most likely to be involved."

"I don't know if anybody from that family is involved." She stared off in the distance, then frowned. "It's been an ugly day." And then filled them in on the recent events.

Carter watched her face, seeing something she wasn't sharing. "And you think you know who's involved"

"Maybe," she said cautiously, "but I can't be sure. I don't want to say anything and be wrong."

"Who are you thinking?" Gordon asked.

"Slim. I fired him this morning."

"Well, that was long overdue."

"It was, indeed," she said, "but you know it won't be that easy." Hailey sat down, her fingers tapping out a pattern on the table as she thought.

Carter watched her process and marveled at the brain behind those eyes. His buddy Gordon was simple, a man of the land. He liked good food, good people, good friends, and had absolutely no interest in business matters. Business was Hailey's forte. She ran the business part of the ranch and was also a partner in her own finance company. A move that had seemed strategic at the time, if a little expensive, but now appeared to be even more profitable.

"And, of course, you'll become one of the prime suspects," Carter pointed out. "If anybody had something against you ..."

She glanced at Gordon.

He frowned and nodded.

"What are you not telling me?" Carter asked. When he got no answer from either of them, he asked another question. "And who is Manfred? I thought I heard his name mentioned somewhere."

"Donnie's boy. Donnie is David's bother. David Longfellow. David and his wife had three daughters," Hailey said quietly. "Almost everyone in town is related to the Longfellows."

Gordon shrugged. "Donnie owns land beside us. He lived here for years, then moved to town once he lost his wife. Since then, Manfred moved in, and we're having some issues with them on land boundaries."

"And water rights, land, animals, you name it," Hailey answered. "They own one hundred acres bordering ours. We've got twice that amount. We're forever dealing with cut fences, their animals mixing with ours, and all kinds of stuff. We had peace and quiet for a long time. Then it just seems like nothing but shit—left, right, and center."

"Is the sheriff doing anything about it?"

"Says he can't do a lot, unless we catch them in the act of vandalizing or stealing our cattle. This is some of the oldest kinds of fights between ranchers ever," Gordon said. "It's one of the reasons I patrol that fence on a regular basis."

"One of the reasons I suggested we put a second fence back a bit and leave that disputed land alone," Hailey said, then pointed to Gordon. "But he thinks they'll just come forward and start cutting the new fence too."

"Why wouldn't they?" Carter said. "If it worked once, it'll work twice. Bullies 101."

"Exactly," Gordon said. He put down his fork, pushed back his empty plate, and grabbed two thick pieces of toasted bread. "You be careful," he told Hailey. "You know what that family is like."

CHAPTER 3

AILEY NODDED. "I know. I had this innocence about working at the company, working with Fred." She turned to Carter. "Fred was such a good man that it made me blind to some of the undercurrents going on around us here at the ranch and also in town. It hadn't occurred to me that this Longfellow clan would be impacting me personally."

"It also takes a strong motive to kill someone so well-loved in a town like this, as you said Fred was," Carter stated. "And then to throw the blame on somebody else. Why would they have chosen Fred over Phil?"

"Good question," she said. "Fred was the founding partner in the business. He was older and had more money, more power, and was a lot better liked than Phil."

"So," Carter continued, "Fred's death would make the ranchers and the town even angrier. And, if they turned on you, that would make your life even worse, right?"

She shot him a startled look. "I don't think I like the way you think."

"No, maybe not. How is your standing in town?"

"The same as always," she said smoothly. "It's only with you that I seem to have a temper."

"Maybe you need to take a look at the people around you and get more of that temper up because somebody seems to be trying to screw you around."

"I doubt anyone in my circle had anything to do with Fred's death."

"Maybe," he said, "but I'm more concerned about Phil."

"So am I." Just then Hailey's phone rang. She answered it to learn the sheriff was heading back to his office. She agreed to meet him there in thirty minutes. She stood, pocketed her phone.

"Are you going to tell him?" Gordon asked.

She shoved her hands in her pockets and nodded. "I don't know what else to do."

"The problem with that though," Gordon added, "is that Raleigh is related to the Longfellows as well, right?"

"I forgot that." Hailey winced. "It's a very tenuous connection."

"That's the problem with this town," Gordon continued. "Everybody has intermarried to the point we're all connected."

"Except you two, correct?" Carter asked Gordon and Hailey. "You two have been here forever, but, Gordon, you didn't marry a Longfellow. Debbie came from out of town. And neither did your father marry into the Longfellow clan."

"I know," Hailey said. "Honestly, even after being born and raised here, I still feel like I'm an outsider." Hailey left the men to meet the sheriff.

As she drove into town, Carter's words rumbled in the back of her head. The problem with people like the Longfellows was how they were an insidious kind of poison. They were the original town founders and thought they were above the law and everyone else, yet always pretended to be good law-abiding citizens. Something was just slimy about the entire group, and she knew she'd have a hard time being nonjudgmental. As she pulled into the parking lot of the sheriff's department, Raleigh pulled up beside her. He smiled as they both exited their vehicles and went inside. He motioned her into his office.

She looked around before saying, "Nobody can overhear us in here?"

He leaned forward. "Nobody can overhear us. Why?"

Hailey hesitated and studied Raleigh. She'd known the man since she was little. She had never had a reason to question his honesty and had never heard any rumors against him. "I'm a little concerned about something I found in the copier at work the other day."

"And you're afraid of who might be involved?"

"Yes," she said. "And, of course, you're related to them."

Raleigh frowned and shuffled the papers on his desk. "I would hope my integrity never comes into question, particularly concerning that family. Three generations of them exist now. The younger ones are always on the edge of crossing the law. I have jailed several members. And we have something like four lawsuits and two court cases coming up against them." He clasped his fingers and added, "The older generation has cleaned up their act as they've aged. No problems with them in eons."

She laughed. "Don't you just love family?"

He shook his head. "Some family, yes. Not *that* family. Now, what's this about?"

She reached into her purse and pulled out two of the sheets of paper she'd found days ago and had copied several times over, along with digitizing them. She laid them both on his desk.

"What am I looking at?"

"Two similar pages, each from two different ledgers, one

which looks doctored. One seems to be the original, and somebody is making changes on a second one."

He frowned at that.

"The two pages contain the same basic items, just the numeric amounts have been tweaked. One page's prices are well over six figures, and the difference between the two books is sixty thousand dollars. For all I know, it's tax evasion or embezzling."

Raleigh sat back and continued to stare at the pages. "Or money laundering."

"Right, so definitely something else to keep in mind when investigating Fred's murder."

Raleigh asked, "When did this happen?"

"Just the other day," she answered. "Friday, last week."

He looked up at her, his eyebrows rising. "Interesting timing."

"Exactly why I'm worried," she said.

"I'll take a copy of these."

"Those copies are for you."

"Were you coming to talk to me about these?" he asked curiously.

"I had already approached Fred about this. I would have talked to him again this morning," she said, "but somebody got to him before I could."

He winced at that. "And you think it's related?"

"I don't know. When a murder happens to one of the three partners within the company, you have to question how it *couldn't* be related."

"Right." He nodded.

She hesitated, then asked, "I know you can't tell me much yet, but did you find anything that pointed to a suspect?"

"No, and they haven't found your missing partner either."

She sank in the chair. "Did you do a home welfare check?"

Raleigh nodded. "The deputy went and knocked. No answer."

She frowned. "Did he look in the windows or anything?"

He shook his head. "I'll make a trip over there myself after this." He checked his watch. "Like right now."

"Can I come?"

He frowned at her. "How about I go first?"

"I've been in their house before. I know his wife. I have no problem walking through the house to see if something's wrong."

"I should go alone, make it an official investigation."

"This *is* official," she said. "One of my partners is dead, and the other's missing. We have to find him." She bolted to her feet. "I'll meet you at Phil's house."

She didn't let Raleigh respond. She hurried to the parking lot, then drove off. She was a mess right now. It wasn't like they had a board of directors to worry about, but they had worse. Their multimillion-dollar clients themselves. This drama would definitely hit their bottom line. More than that, she was afraid it would hit her personally too. It was bad enough she'd already lost her friend. It was even worse to think somebody might have done this to frame her. If so, even just the hint of that could ruin her reputation in her field.

Phil didn't live far out. As Hailey turned into his driveway, she scanned his place for any sign his vehicle was in the garage. Or if he had at least gotten home last night. They had checked his office but hadn't checked his planner, after

all. For all she knew, he'd taken a day off and gone somewhere. He'd been a little off lately anyway. She had asked
him if he was okay, but he had just shrugged and gave her a
smile, saying he was tired. Hailey tried her best to think
positive and even thought about how much Phil wouldn't
appreciate it if somebody broke into his house, even if to
check on him. Still, they needed to know if he was dead or
injured. She winced. So much for thinking positive.

She parked her car and ran to the garage door. It was
unlocked. When she opened it, she found Phil's and Betty's
cars inside. Hailey's heart raced. She rushed to the inner
door, finding it unlocked as well, and raced inside the house,
not minding that the sheriff was still a few paces behind her.
She stepped into the kitchen and walked in a frenzy through
the main floor. She found no sign of anyone. When she
heard Raleigh at the front door, she opened it for him.

"The garage door wasn't locked. And the inside garage
door was unlocked too," she told him. "I see no sign of a
struggle—no sign of anyone in the whole ground floor. Both
cars are in the garage."

"Stay here."

Hailey's hands shook, and she paced about as she
watched Raleigh climb the stairs to the bedrooms. She saw
him enter the spare rooms by the bathroom. Then he
disappeared from her line of sight. She waited on pins and
needles. She stopped breathing and counted for a minute.
She exhaled. Two minutes. Still no Raleigh.

She bolted to the stairs, worried someone might be holding Phil prisoner and now the sheriff too. She knew it was
foolish, and she also knew Carter and her brother would yell
at her if they knew, but she had to do it.

The master bedroom door was closed when she reached

that room, and she cursed under her breath. She approached it in caution and put her ear against the door. She heard nothing. But then the door opened abruptly and revealed the sheriff, who stepped back in surprise.

"When you didn't come back," Hailey said, "I was afraid somebody held Phil and his wife and now you hostage."

"No, thank heavens," he said, but his voice was harsh, and his face was drawn. "But you won't have to worry about a second partner. Phil and his wife are in there, … and they've both been shot dead."

She stared at him, falling back against the railing. "What?" she croaked. "Are you serious?"

"It looks to be a murder-suicide."

"But why?" she cried out.

"I don't know. I found no suicide note. I'm waiting for my team to arrive."

Hailey took several staggering steps, then turned to look at him. "As in, maybe Phil shot Fred first, then came home to shoot his wife and himself?"

"If that was the case, he would have taken the gun, don't you think?"

"Unless he shot Fred and then remembered he'd left the gun in the wrong hand and realized he was likely to get caught, so he took out his wife and himself?" Hailey's words came out in a rush. She honestly didn't know what else to think. Her mind ran wild with a hundred thoughts per minute. It felt like everything was falling apart, and she couldn't do much about it. She badly wished she could have some semblance of normalcy.

"And now we're just reaching," Raleigh said gently. "Go home. I'll come to the ranch as soon as I can."

She forced herself to nod. Her head felt heavy and stiff.

"Like those two sheets you showed me, who had access to all your client accounts?" the sheriff called after her as she walked downstairs.

She looked up at him and answered in a barely audible voice. "All three of us. All three of us had access. We were partners."

"Well, guess what?" Raleigh's voice was harsher than she would have liked to hear. "You now own it all."

When she stepped out of the house, slamming the door hard behind her, she burst into tears.

DRIVING THROUGH TOWN, Carter headed toward the airport. It was small but busy. There, he talked to some of the baggage handlers and asked about the fate of the dog. One man was open and willing to answer any questions, while another just shook his head and told Carter to talk to management. Carter took that to mean, if there were a lawsuit, that employee wouldn't be part of it. However, the first man had made it clear that the dog had arrived, but the Longfellows hadn't been there to pick it up.

"Did they come at all?"

"I can't tell you," the first man said. "I was off to lunch by then. But I can tell you that they weren't waiting when I got back to work. The dog looked pretty exhausted too."

"Long trip for him," Carter said. "What happens if a dog's not claimed?"

"It would go to animal rescue. They'll hold on to it and make queries. In this case, I don't know what happened. I imagine the sheriff would have been contacted. Surely someone made inquiries. The Longfellows didn't receive the dog, so they don't likely know anything about its fate."

"But they said the dog didn't arrive."

"I heard that too," the cooperative baggage handler said with a snort. "What probably happened is they arrived late, and somebody had moved the dog. Then they took that as an easy excuse to disappear."

Carter had to wonder. "Do you know who was on the shipping label as the person to contact for pickup?"

The attendant frowned. "I think—but don't quote me on this—I think it was Brenda Longfellow. Good luck trying to get answers out of the Longfellows. If there's credit to be taken, they'll take it, even if they don't deserve it. But if there's blame to be handed out? You could bet they won't be anywhere near close by."

Carter watched in amusement as the man walked away. He had an interesting attitude and one that also mirrored Gordon's. Now, what the heck was Carter supposed to do with this? It was an interesting conundrum because the Longfellows were supposedly a well-respected family—one of the founding families in the city—and yet those who did business with them considered them sleazy, cheap, unethical, and downright on the edge of being illegal. And likely over the edge but with enough legal coverage to keep their asses out of jail. Apparently several lawyers were in the family too, which made life convenient for them. Were they all bad? Or, like many families, was one arm worse than the rest?

Carter needed intel, so he called Geir. Mostly to confirm the names of the players here.

"David Longfellow," Geir replied.

"Yeah, that's what I have down."

"On the form here, we also have a Brenda Longfellow."

"Right, she's the contact for the adoption. I wonder if

she and David are husband and wife."

"Generally these dogs are only given to families," Geir said, "or couples, to give some stability to the dog."

"Okay, good. Now at least we know who we need to talk to."

"I'll send you images of the adoption form application, in case you can use anything on it. It's got all the info there."

"Thanks," Carter said. Then he hung up and waited. Sure enough, he received several photos of the entire form. With that information, he dialed Brenda. He identified who he was when she picked up her phone.

"Oh my," Brenda said. "That was such a long time ago."

"It was just a few months ago," he said in a dry tone.

"Well, it seems like a long time ago. We never got the dog. I don't know why you keep calling."

"According to the airport handlers, the dog did arrive."

An odd silence came on the other end of the call. "I'm not sure what you're implying," she said slowly, "but we would not have left the dog to his own devices at the airport. We take our responsibilities very seriously."

"The dog was left for one full hour after the time it arrived. What time did you go to pick him up?"

"I'm not sure I could tell you," Brenda said in an off-hand way. "I didn't go myself. I sent one of my staff to pick it up."

"Do you know what time that was?"

"It certainly would have been before the dog arrived. The animals are taken off the plane quickly. We would have been out of there in no time."

"When did you realize you didn't have the dog?"

"When the driver came back, of course," she said in exasperation. "I don't know what you expect to do about it now. Obviously somebody took the dog for himself."

"Any idea who would want to?"

"No clue. I'm sure I can't tell you anything more. Now, I'm only talking to you as a courtesy, so I'd appreciate the same courtesy back."

That shot his eyebrows up because, as far as he was concerned, he was being very polite. "Of course. It's just that the US Navy's War Dogs division is eager to find out what happened to their dog."

"I can't believe they sent somebody in person!"

"Could I speak with the staff member who went to pick up the dog?"

There came that same silence, only this time it was a little more fraught with worry. "I'll have him contact you. That's the best I can do." She hung up on him.

Carter stared at his phone and frowned. He went inside a nearby coffee shop, ordered a coffee, pulled open his laptop, and hooked up to their Wi-Fi to research the Longfellow family.

When a young woman brought his coffee, she smiled. "Are you looking for Brenda and David?"

"I just spoke to Brenda," he said, carefully moving the laptop ever-so-slightly to the side so she couldn't see the screen.

"Ah, well, it wouldn't take long to find them anyway. They're involved in everything here."

"You know them well?"

"No," she said, "but I know of them. Everyone does."

"Right."

"My brother knows the family too," she said abruptly. Something odd was in her tone.

"That doesn't sound good."

"My brother got into trouble with one of them. Then my brother got suspended from school."

"Ouch."

She nodded. "Ouch is true. We're trying to get him back in again, so he can finish his education."

"What happened?"

"They said he punched a kid. One of their family."

"One of the Longfellows?"

She nodded. "Burgess Longfellow goes to the same school."

"Did your brother hit him?"

She looked him straight in the face and nodded. "He did. He had a damn good reason."

"Sorry about that," Carter said. "It seems a little too often that people with influence win out, even over justice."

Her shoulders seemed to sag a little as she relaxed. She glanced around the empty coffee shop. "You just have to watch out who you talk to in this town. It's very much a 70/30 split. Seventy percent of the population are all for the Longfellows, while thirty are against them."

"Why do the Longfellows rate so high?"

"Because they're in politics. They're into the businesses big-time here. Own this whole town and all our jobs. Everybody wants to rub shoulders with them and hope for a little bit of help when they need various permits and stuff."

"Do they take bribes?"

"Of course they do," she said, but then she backtracked. "I don't actually know if they do or not. It just seems to me that they're the kind of people who would. Definitely sleazy. Not my kind of people at all."

"Sounds like you and your brother have a good head on your shoulders. He just needs to return to school to finish up and stay away from this Burgess."

"Yeah, he does, but it's easier said than done. The Long-fellows are trying to make sure my brother can't go back."

Carter's eyebrows rose. "I don't like the sound of that."

She gave him a half smile. "None of us do. But, if the Longfellows say so, then my brother won't have a leg to stand on."

At the ring of the bells on the front door, she turned and walked away. Carter glanced around to see a group of men walking into the coffee shop. Watching the interaction between her and them, he realized they were the reason she backed off. And not just to get their order. So, they were either important or connected.

He went back to his research on the Longfellow family. Carter found many twisted litigations and some pending lawsuits against the Longfellows, mostly for not yet fully paying their contractors. Apparently, in the past, the Longfellows liked to do large property building deals and then screwed the construction people out of most of their payments due. Carter didn't have much truck with that. As a matter of fact, he had none. That was just a shit move. Still, no information showed up on recent property deals.

However, when he did a search for a family tree, that brought up an interesting set of relationships. Multiple marriages, almost no divorces, with many grandchildren, and the grandparents were still alive. This particular genealogy tree was four years old, so there had likely been further changes. It proved a fascinating but terribly unhelpful read.

Carter saved several other pages and then studied the application download on his phone again. Apparently the Longfellows were *true patriots* and had a lot of experience breeding dogs—on paper anyway. He almost laughed at that.

Since when did being a patriot become a requirement for looking after a retired War Dog?

He thought about all the other War Dogs who had hopefully retired and wondered how many had gone terribly wrong and ended up in the hands of these fake patriots and shook his head. Of course he didn't know the number of files where the retired War Dog had been successfully placed and confirmed in a random wellness visit some time later. That meant the government's data on these War Dogs was skewed and unreliable.

When the waitress came back around, she refilled his coffee with a brief smile and disappeared before he could say anything. Likely deliberate on her part too. He shrugged. As he was about to close his laptop, his phone rang. It was Brenda.

"Yes, hello. My driver is in town at the moment. You can talk to him outside the hardware store in ten minutes, if that's okay."

As it was likely to be all the opportunity he would get, he gave his assent. "I'm in the coffee shop right now. I'll be there as soon as I find out where the hardware store is."

"Down the end of Main Street," she said before hanging up.

He paid for his coffee, thanked the girl, looked at the three men sitting with their heads bent together, and headed to the truck he'd borrowed from the ranch. He wished he could have taken the men's photo, but he needed to be discreet. Plus he was in a rush.

On the way to the parking lot outside the coffee shop, he found a Lexus and a fully loaded three-quarter-ton diesel truck. He took photos of those license plates before sending them off to Geir. No doubt they were Longfellow owned.

Hopping into Gordon's truck and heading to Main Street, Carter vaguely remembered where the hardware store was.

When he finally reached it, he got out, walked around, and waited. He didn't even know what the man looked like that he was meeting. But then nobody was here. He frowned, wondering if he'd been stiffed, when an old truck pulled into the corner lot. The man got out and headed toward the hardware store.

Carter stopped him. "Do you work for Brenda?"

The man nodded, pushing his beaten hat off his head. "Do I know you?"

"Probably not, but I've been around lots over the last fifteen years. I'm here on behalf of the War Dogs department."

A nervous look shot across the man's face. He shoved his hands into his pockets. "And?"

"According to Brenda, you were the one who went to pick up Matzuka, the War Dog. Is that correct?"

"That's correct."

"Did you see the dog?"

"Nope, I told Brenda it wasn't there when I arrived at the airport."

"I know that's what you told Brenda," he said in a gentle tone. "But, like I said, I'm from the US Navy's War Dogs Department. And I'm looking for the truth."

The man nervously backed up half a step.

"I don't necessarily have to tell that truth to Brenda," Carter said.

The man snorted and spat on the ground. "No matter what anybody says, everything goes back to them. I went to the airport to pick up the dog. The dog wasn't there. I told

Brenda. Then I went home. That's all there is to it."

"How close to arrival time did you get there?"

"I was there before arrival time. I stayed for an hour before leaving."

"Are two airports here? According to the baggage handler at one, that dog sat there, waiting for a pickup, for a full hour after he'd arrived."

"There's only one airport, and the baggage handler lied. But what else is new?"

"Meaning, everybody here lies?"

"They're either lying for one side or the other," the man said, his face twisted in a bitter way. "Now, excuse me. I need to go into the hardware store. I could lose my job if I'm late."

He watched the old guy go in. One of the witnesses was flat-out lying, but who? Who had more motivation to lie, the driver or the baggage handler? Carter leaned against the ranch truck and called Geir.

"Interesting scenario there," Geir said, after Carter told him the story.

"Yeah."

"And who do you think is lying?"

"I think the delivery driver, but I'm not sure why. I don't know if he picked up the dog and didn't want anybody to know the Longfellows have him or if he didn't pick up the dog and didn't want to acknowledge what might have happened to Matzuka."

"Very strange. Do you have any names for me?"

Carter gave him the name of the baggage handler. "The second guy at the airport told me to talk to management. He wouldn't give me any answers. Oh, but I did have an interesting conversation with a woman working at a coffee shop."

"Go on."

He explained what the girl had said about her brother getting kicked out of school because of Burgess Longfellow.

"Wow, okay," Geir said. "So, we have a fairly small-town family who's grown too big for its britches and is now calling all the shots. And somehow we allowed a War Dog to go to *that* family."

"According to this application form, the Longfellows said they're breeders and have trainers on the property. I don't think these people would even dirty their hands with dogs, but I don't know that. I'm presuming Matzuka was fixed because he was a War Dog, right?"

"Yes. Standard procedure."

"So he was no good for breeding," Carter said.

"No. Unless they're grabbing his genes: But I don't know why they would do that. That's very expensive. Plus other dogs are easier to get a hold of."

"I think Brenda was correct in saying she didn't get the dog. I'm not sure why she wanted it in the first place. Unless it was for the prestige alone."

"If the prestige was so important to her, why didn't she report the dog missing? Why didn't she follow up? Unless she realized she made a mistake and was grateful for an out."

"Maybe. Or she didn't realize that the government was going to keep an eye on the dog. That might have caused her a hasty retreat on the deal," Carter said. "I'm not sure the Longfellow mind-set is rational."

"But was the driver correct in saying he didn't pick it up?" Geir asked. "That's what we have to track down."

"That's a good point," Carter said. "My take is that, if the baggage handler was correct, and he said the dog was there for a full hour, then the delivery guy was somewhere else and had to cover his tracks in order to not get in trouble with Brenda. If that's the case, we need to find out what he was really doing, where he was, and what happened to the dog at that time."

"I'll phone the local sheriff there," Geir replied. "I want them to know we have some government officials looking into this. Although this is off the books, it's still as official as I can make it."

Carter looked up just in time to see the delivery guy walk out of the hardware store. The man had a bag in his hand, and he tossed it into the front seat of his truck before he got in. Before he could turn on the engine though, Carter stood right beside him. "You didn't tell me the truth. I don't believe you were at the airport at the time you were supposed to be. I'll check the video cameras, but you might want to give me a better explanation now. And I promise it won't go to Brenda."

The old man glared at him. "I need this job."

"Did you hear me? It won't go back to Brenda."

"Everything goes back to Brenda."

"Did you have to see the doctor or did something else happen? Did your truck break down? What happened?" Carter fired question after question, hoping to disarm the older man.

"My granddaughter was in trouble," he said. "I had to help her. When I got to the airport, the dog wasn't there."

"But the official story you gave Brenda is that you got there on time and that you stayed for an hour, then called her to say you saw no sign of the dog, correct?"

He nodded. "But, if Brenda ever asks me about it, I'll tell her that you lied."

"Good enough. But I still need to find out where the dog is. Have you seen or heard of anybody having it?"

He shook his head. "No, but I know an awful lot of animal rights activists are around. If anybody had thought that dog stayed caged up for too long, they might have just opened the cage door and let it go."

At that, Carter straightened and stared at him in horror. "And then what?"

"Then the dog's gone." The man shrugged. "Who knows where or how it's living?"

"Would anybody report a stray dog on its own?"

"No, they'll more likely put a bullet in its head, thinking it would come after their livestock."

"But it would have been released at the airport, so it's hard to say where it could be now."

"It could also have gotten into somebody's vehicle, or it could have been picked up by somebody. I've got no clue. I just know that, when I was there, I saw no sign of the dog."

"And you're not lying now?"

"No."

"What about your granddaughter? Is she okay?"

Surprise lit the old man's eyes. "She will be. But she'll be a hell of a lot better off when she's away from this town. She got tangled in a Longfellow mess."

"Anyone in particular?"

"Burgess. Kid's a piece of shit. Takes what he wants and doesn't care who says no."

At that, Carter felt a wave of old anger rising up. "Did he hurt her?"

"She managed to get free, but she's pretty shaken up, and she'll miss the next term of school."

"That's the second kid I've heard of who Burgess took

65

out of school. Any point in talking to the sheriff?"

"It's her word against his. Everybody in this damn town will side with the Longfellows."

"Not necessarily Burgess though. Once he crosses a line, he can get slapped into jail too."

"And the Longfellows just buy his way back out again. I don't know if the sheriff's any good, but I know most of the law is in the Longfellows' pocket. You can't trust any of them."

With that, the driver turned on the engine and drove away. Noting the license plate, Carter walked back to Gordon's truck, thinking about Hailey and the mess she was dealing with. And the sheriff. What if the sheriff also had something to do with those family members? What would happen to the supposed suicide investigation into Fred's death? Not knowing what kind of reception he would get, he pulled out his phone and called Hailey. However, when she answered, he could hear the tears in her voice. "What happened? Are you okay? Are you hurt?"

She sniffled several times to clear her throat. "I will be okay, but my other partner, Phil, is dead too. So is his wife."

Everything inside Carter clenched tight. In a harsh voice, he asked, "Where are you now?"

"I'm still at their place. The sheriff's here with every-one." Then she added in a whisper, "I don't know what to do anymore."

"Sit still. I'm coming."

"Don't bother. I'll go straight home."

"I want to talk to the sheriff. A couple of the locals aren't so sure he's squeaky clean. Apparently a lot of the deputies in town are from the Longfellow clan."

"Oh, they are," she said. "If they aren't family, they're

likely being bought off by the family. I don't think the sheriff's the same though. I already had a discussion with him about that."

"Maybe. But do you know if there's any relationship between your Slim guy and Burgess?"

"Brothers. I think about twelve years is between them. And they are David's grandsons, so also Longfellows."

"How old is Burgess?"

"Seventeenish, but he acts like a kid. If there was ever a bully in a sandbox, it's him."

"And Slim is almost thirty?"

"Or is thirty," she said. Fatigue was in her voice. "Why?"

"Burgess attacked a young woman—the granddaughter of one of the delivery men who works for Brenda and was supposed to pick up the dog. According to the baggage handler, the dog was sitting at the airport for over an hour. But the delivery guy told Brenda that he was there before the dog arrived and stayed a full hour, yet never saw the dog. And that's because he was trying to help his granddaughter, who had just gotten free from Burgess's attack."

"Bastard," she said with heat. "That little piece of shit needs to have his ass kicked into tomorrow."

"I also spoke to a waitress at the coffee shop here ..."

"Sonia."

"Okay. Yeah, her brother was suspended from school because of Burgess. Apparently her brother hit Burgess."

"Good for him."

"Maybe, but it sounds like those kids won't be allowed back into school."

CHAPTER 4

"THAT'S JUST WRONG," Hailey exclaimed. "I can't believe how the Longfellows are allowed to run this town."

"I know it's been a couple years since I was here, but I don't remember hearing anything about this."

"We didn't have anything to do with the family until Manfred took over the property next to us."

"Do you know where Debbie is?"

She snorted at that. "Why? Will you plead my brother's cause?"

"No, I'd like to tell her to come home and to kick Gordon's ass," he said. "I already had a talk with him about that this morning and last night."

She laughed but it wasn't the happy kind. "I don't think it'll do any good. He's too set in his ways."

"But I like Debbie too. I want to say hi."

"She's working at the insurance company. Stop in and say hi. Watch out though. The Longfellows own the insurance company."

After hanging up on Carter, Hailey stood and brushed off her pants, then took a Kleenex and blew her nose. She also wiped her eyes, waved goodbye to the sheriff, leaving Phil's house, and got into her truck. Maybe she'd be able to drive now. But she was pretty rough still as she drove out the driveway. She had to get out of the way for the coroner to come in. She avoided town and headed home.

As soon as she hopped out, her brother came outside, eating fresh bread covered in peanut butter. "Is that lunch or dinner for you?" she asked him.

He shrugged. "Wasn't sure what was going on with anybody. I just needed a snack."

"Phil's dead too," she said abruptly.

Gordon stared at her and slowly lowered his hand with the bread. "How?"

"It's supposed to look like he came home and shot his wife and then himself. Maybe that's what happened. I don't know."

"So Betty's dead too?"

Hailey nodded. "And that leaves me as the only remaining partner."

"Which makes you the number one murder suspect."

"Yes. But another thought occurred to me. Maybe I'm next."

"Jesus!" Gordon grabbed her arm and pulled her into the house. "Are you in danger?"

She shrugged her shoulders. "How the hell am I supposed to know? Just think about it. Two partners are dead. One theory is, Phil went to work, shot Fred, and made it look like a suicide. But, when he got home, he realized he made a mistake leaving the gun in the wrong hand, and, therefore, people would know it was murder. He would get caught, so maybe he shot Betty first and then himself. I don't know. As much as I would hate that to be true, I almost prefer it to any of the other options."

"What other options?" Gordon's voice was hard.

"That somebody shot all three."

"What have you gotten yourself into, sis?"

"I don't know," she said, walking through to the living room and throwing herself across the couch. "It's just too unbelievable to even contemplate."

"You know that the sheriff will be all over this."

"You mean, they'll be all over me? Yes, I know."

"And that other thought you brought up? Well, that's just too horrible. What's the chance it's a valid possibility?"

She laughed. "Ask the killer. I don't know. Maybe he's done now. Maybe Phil killed the others. Maybe he and Fred had a big falling out. I don't know. All I know is both my partners are dead, and I have a company to run that apparently I now own."

"And, if something happens to you, what happens to the company?"

"Again, I can't tell you. I have to take a look at the legal documents. I'm not sure we ever put in a contingency plan, in case all three of us died at once. It's not a normal circumstance."

"No, but you need to take a look at it now," he said. "*Today*. And you need to contact your lawyer and settle it up because, if somebody is hoping you die too, or if somebody else has decided to step in and make sure they do a clean sweep, does it go to the rest of the employees? Does it get sold and then split by the remaining family members of the three partners? Just what happens?"

"As soon as I can get the energy to sit back up again, I'll grab my laptop and start looking."

"I can do one better than that." Gordon snagged Hailey's laptop from her bag and handed it to her. Then he went back and grabbed her mouse. "Start looking because we have to head this off right now."

"I know. I was just trying to avoid any further ugly discussions for at least five minutes."

"Is the sheriff coming here today?"

"I imagine so, but honestly his hands are pretty full."

"Jesus, poor Betty. She had nothing to do with any of this."

"I know. And the same goes for you."

Gordon looked startled. "You think I'm in danger too?"

"I have no clue."

Hailey opened her laptop and brought up the partnership's legal documents. Everything was backed up in cloud storage, where she could get them fairly quickly. As she read through them, she realized nothing was really in place as a safeguard in case all three of them died. She reached for her cell phone and phoned her lawyer. Of course he was busy. She talked to Louise, his clerk, and said she needed him to phone her back as soon as possible.

Louise agreed. "I guess this is about Fred, isn't it?"

"Just tell him to call me," Hailey said, then hung up and turned to her brother. "Nobody knows about Phil yet, but it won't take long."

"I know," he said. "That's why we need the lawyer."

She gave a strangled laugh. "But, of course, he's busy."

"Always. Just keep on him."

As she thought about it, she realized the lawyer needed to get off whatever the hell he was doing and contact her. She picked up the phone and redialed.

When Louise answered again, she said, "I don't know where he is."

"But I need to talk to him right now," Hailey insisted.

The secretary sighed. "He's in a meeting."

"I doubt it. He's probably sitting there with his feet up

on the desk."

"Same difference," Louise snapped. "Look. I have to follow what he tells me to say. If I want to keep my job, that is."

"I'd appreciate it if you would find him."

"Just a moment."

Louise put her on hold, and Hailey didn't know if she would really check up on the lawyer or not, but, just a few minutes later, Charlie's voice came on the phone.

"What's up, and why the panic?"

"You heard about Fred, right?"

His voice lowered as he answered, "Yeah, I did. I'm so sorry about that."

"Are you alone in your office?"

"I am. Louise just left."

"Did she close the door?"

She could almost visualize him straightening in his chair. "Yes. What's up?"

"Phil is dead too."

Stunned silence filled the phone lines for a moment. "What?"

"He was either murdered or it was suicide. Either way, he's dead."

"Good Lord."

"I'm looking at the partnership documents right now. If Phil was murdered too, that's two partners murdered. I don't know if I'm next, but we don't have any contingency in place for the company if all three partners die."

"Are you sure?"

Hailey imagined he was opening his own set of documents now.

"Are you afraid for your own life?" Charlie asked.

"We're not sure what's going on, but it doesn't matter whether I'm murdered or I get behind the wheel and die in a true accident. What matters is the contingency plan. There's none in place."

"What do you want to do then?"

She gave a harsh laugh. "I have no clue. What suggestions do you have?"

"Well, at the moment, the company is 100 percent yours, based on the contract we put into place last year. And, of course, we never thought *this* would happen."

"I know," she said. "Phil and Betty had a foster daughter, Angela. They got her later in life, then had some bigger issues with her when she came of age, and they definitely had a parting of the ways when she starting going out with Walton Longfellow, one of the deputies in town. That was a relationship they didn't approve of. I don't think they had much to do with her lately, even though the two split up. Although it's a moot point now as both Phil and his wife are dead."

"Betty too?" The lawyer's voice escalated.

"Yes," she said. "And, of course, Fred's wife died a long time ago."

"Which makes you a very wealthy woman," Charlie said.

"If I live to see it. I didn't want to become a wealthy woman through the death of my friends."

"No, of course not," he said, his voice subdued. "Okay, I'm writing up a draft. But you need to tell me who you want the company to go to, in case you're killed."

She stared at her brother. "My brother would probably hate me for it, but let's add him there."

Gordon glared at her. "Don't you dump that on me. I don't know anything about finance."

"I don't know anybody else who's good at finance." She saw a grin flash across his face. "Now what?"

"Except for one person," Gordon said. "Who you don't like."

She stared at him. "Who are you talking about?"

"Carter."

"Carter's a military man," she snapped. "And a carpenter and a jack-of-all-trades."

"Have you forgotten who helped you when you were running into trouble with some of your finance courses?"

She sagged onto the couch and stared at her brother. "He has a degree in finance, doesn't he?"

Gordon's grin widened.

"Jesus." She shook her head. "I'll have to think about that. He's been out of the loop for so long."

"But you have to leave it to somebody," the voice in her ear said. "So how about this guy and Gordon? Do they know each other?"

"Best friends," she said.

"So, leave it to both of them, and they can help each other out."

A part of her heart laughed because, in a way, it was the perfect revenge on Carter, who hated even the idea of a desk job. But, at the same time, it was also potentially a smart move. She gave Charlie the two names he needed. "Go ahead and do it. Send me the documents and make sure your secretary has no way of knowing about this conversation. The sheriff has already made it clear that I'm not allowed to broadcast Phil's death."

"Of course not," Charlie said, "but you're allowed to talk to your lawyer."

"Too bad you're not a criminal lawyer," she said, a note

of hysteria entering her voice, "because I might need one."

"They don't suspect you, do they?"

"Who else will they suspect? They always look to the family and partners first. I just gained a company."

"And you're the youngest member."

"I know." She groaned "but I didn't have anything to do with it."

"Then trust in the law." He paused before speaking again. "And maybe you need a criminal lawyer who doesn't live in town. I know what the law is like here too."

"Which is why you moved," she said. "If you were still here, I wouldn't be using you."

"Let me get this done. I'll handle this personally and fire the documents off to you. Hold tight for ten minutes."

She hung up and contemplated the sudden shift in her life.

"Is he writing something up?" Gordon asked.

"*I'll handle it personally*," she mimed.

"So this alone should cost you ten grand."

"Not quite," she said. "But, if I am taken out of the picture, it might give us a better idea of who's doing it."

Gordon stood in front of her. "I don't want to hear you talking about something like that."

"I heard the last part of that but not all of it," Carter said from the doorway. "Why a lawyer?"

"The company is now hers," Gordon said, "but they had no documentation in place if something happens to her too."

"Is that what you now suspect?" Carter's worried gaze went from Gordon to Hailey and back. "That two members have been taken out, so the third one is the next target?"

"Maybe," Hailey said.

"But what would happen if nobody was there to take

over the company?"

CARTER COULDN'T BELIEVE what had just happened to Hailey. "It makes no sense," he said.

"Unless it was a murder-suicide," she said. She hopped up and walked into the kitchen, and in a furious set of motions began making some big vegetable salad. He watched her knife flash with an angry precision and realized it was just to give her something to do. However, in the mood she was in, he wasn't sure if it was a good thing or not. He exchanged a glance with Gordon, who just shrugged.

"Let's hope the sheriff can get to the bottom of this fast," Gordon said.

Hailey scoffed. "Even if he does, you know what the rest of the town'll say."

"Doesn't matter what they say. You and I both know that this isn't something to play around with. People will talk. It's not something that'll affect you."

"Says you," she said. "They were my friends. And I really liked them. Particularly Fred. He was a good man. He didn't deserve to die this way."

"Phil wasn't looking very well the last time I saw him," Gordon said.

She stopped chopping for a moment, as if to consider his words. "You know what? I was thinking the same thing. Maybe that needs to be checked out. Maybe he had terminal cancer or something."

"And then what? He shot his longtime partner and his wife because he didn't want to die alone?"

"I don't know," she said and resumed chopping vegetables again.

"The sheriff will look into that. And speaking of which …" Gordon pointed out the window.

A vehicle came down the driveway, kicking up a nice cloud of dust.

"Is that the sheriff?" Carter asked.

"Probably," Hailey said. "He said he would come here."

She went back to her chopping as if it all had to be done before the sheriff showed up. Carter wondered at her state of mind. But she'd also just lost two friends who were business associates as well and had found the body of one of them. For anybody not used to seeing death, that was traumatic in itself. But, with the rest of this piled on, it could be even worse.

"The sheriff's connected to the Longfellows, correct?" Carter asked.

"In a distant way. I don't even know what the tenuous connection is between all my different staff and my company and the Longfellows. It's something I'll have to take a closer look at."

"Who did the hiring?"

"We haven't hired anybody since I came on," she said. "Except Slim. And I was totally against that."

"Are they all long-term employees?"

"Longer than me, so over four years," she said.

"And, of course, that'll be tough to handle too," Carter said. She shot him a look but enough clarity resided in her expression for him to understand she knew exactly what he was talking about. He watched as the sheriff pulled up beside her truck. The man hopped out and walked toward the door at a steady pace. He looked like a no-nonsense kind of guy. But Carter had also heard the rumors and wasn't too sure how the sheriff's connection to the Longfellows played out.

The sheriff walked into the open door, nodded at Gordon, then looked at Hailey. "You got a few minutes to talk?"

"Talk away," she said. "I keep nothing from my brother."

The sheriff zeroed in on Carter, who leaned against a wall. "And who are you?" he asked with a narrow gaze.

"Carter," he said. "I've met you a couple times over the years, but I think the last time was about three and a half years ago."

The sheriff frowned. "I don't remember." His tone was abrupt, as if he already didn't trust Carter.

Gordon stepped in. "He's been here many times over the last fifteen years. He was in the navy until he was injured and is now out of service."

The sheriff nodded. "Okay, maybe I do remember you." He frowned though, looking from Carter to Gordon and back to Hailey. "Are you sure?"

"Why not? Everybody else in town will be talking."

Raleigh sighed heavily. "It's up to the coroner to make a determination as to whether it was the same killer or not, which will take a while, but I see no logical reason for Phil to have killed Fred."

"You don't know that. None of us do. Also you need to check into Phil's medical records. I think he was quite ill."

Raleigh looked at her for a long moment. "The coroner will do that too."

"What happens now with the company? I own it completely," she said without looking up.

Carter watched the sheriff's face during the whole exchange. It gave nothing away. Raleigh already knew that information.

"Nobody else gets a piece?"

She shook her head. "No, I'm the sole beneficiary, and, therefore, your number one suspect." She picked up her chopping board and dumped all the vegetables into a bowl. "Or the next dead body to show up."

"Can you put that down and give me your full attention?" the sheriff asked.

Hailey slammed down the board and her knife, then turned to glare at him. "How much attention do you want? I didn't kill any of those three people. They were my friends, and I had a lot of respect for both of my partners!"

"What about Betty?"

"I've only met her a handful of times, when we had various company parties and things," she said. "She seemed like a lovely woman, but I didn't know her well."

"Any idea why somebody would target both of your partners?"

"Not outside of the paperwork I showed you today. It's also quite possible Phil's the one who killed Fred and then went home and shot Betty and himself."

"That would make things nice and simple, but there needs to be one hell of a motivator for that."

"Back to his health then. I don't know."

Raleigh looked at Gordon. "I'm asking everybody, so don't be insulted. Do you have an alibi for last night?"

"What time?"

"After six p.m. Right through the night."

Gordon motioned to Carter. "Carter arrived on the 5:36 flight. We three had dinner, then all went to bed, and the morning started all over again, just like it always does."

At the sound of Carter's name, the sheriff looked at him. "Where'd you come in from?"

"New Mexico," he said but didn't offer anything else.

"Just a social visit?"

"Business and pleasure," he said slowly, crossing his arms. "I'm here on behalf of the US Navy's War Dogs program. Sent by Titanium Corp out of New Mexico." He pulled out one of Geir's cards from his wallet. "Feel free to call him and clear me from any of your local crimes. I was going to stop in and ask you about a missing dog as it is."

"A dog?" the sheriff said in disgust.

"A highly trained War Dog that the US military put a lot of money into was supposed to be adopted by Brenda and David Longfellow. However, according to Brenda, they never received the dog. And yet the dog was shipped to the airport here."

The sheriff scratched the hair under his hat. "Well, now ..."

"Apparently nobody reported it missing until the War Dogs division did a follow-up. And found out that supposedly the dog never arrived. Per Brenda anyway."

"Where the hell is it then?" Raleigh asked. "Dogs just don't disappear. Especially not dogs like that."

"Exactly why I'm here," Carter said with the same cool tone. "To find the dog and to find out what happened to him."

"Like I need this shit," the sheriff snapped. "Ah, hell."

"If it had been dealt with weeks ago, it wouldn't have been an issue," Carter said. "The fact that my arrival coincided with a local murder is just that—a coincidence."

The sheriff nodded but didn't look like he believed him. "I'll be phoning your boss to make sure."

"Go for it. I'm sure he'd be delighted to talk to you. You're the local law around here, and a very expensive dog went missing, yet nobody seems to give a shit. He'll want to know any of the relevant information sitting in the case files."

"I don't have any case files. I can't work a crime if nobody reports it."

"Then we should probably go back to Brenda and ask her why she didn't report it."

"That won't do any good, son. I can tell you that now."

"Maybe, but that doesn't stop the fact that military inquiries and local investigations have to be made."

"Now I know who you are. You talked to Brenda today, didn't you?"

"I phoned her, yes," Carter said with a smile. "Did she call you?"

"There's a message on my desk about some stranger bugging her."

Carter laughed. "If asking questions about a highly expensive government dog that she signed on to look after and to keep in good health is *bugging* her, then, yes, that was me. And you can bet her sorry ass I'll be doing a lot more *bugging* until I get to the bottom of it too."

Carter would brook absolutely no interference when he got on a mission. The trouble was, these people didn't know him when he was on the job, and people like Brenda were just irritants along the way. She could make as many complaints as she wanted, but, if she had anything to do with his dog going missing, he would make sure she paid for it.

The sheriff's back went up. "I can't have you harassing Brenda."

"How about I start harassing the rest of her family? Like maybe Slim or that useless kid Burgess who's attacking young women."

"You're opening your mouth about an awful lot of local people here, people who are highly respected. And, if an attack has happened, I haven't heard about it."

"And involving a lot of people who aren't so highly respected, I guess," Carter said. "Like maybe people around here don't trust you."

The sheriff's mouth slowly closed at that. He turned to look at Gordon and Hailey. He didn't look pleased about any of it. "This is a really bad time to be stirring up hornets."

"There's never a good time," Carter said, "unless you catch it right when the hornets are building their nest."

"Well, that time's long past around here." The sheriff slapped the counter. "I'll be going now." He turned and walked away.

Carter looked at Hailey. "Well, that went well."

"No," she said. "He gets leaned on by the Longfellows pretty heavily."

"Maybe," he said, "but, when it comes to the law, he's got to stay legal. To hell with keeping the Longfellows happy."

"I know," she said. "But, like Gordon has told you before, we already have land dispute issues. And we know it's one of them too."

"Have you got anybody to help you guys?"

Gordon puffed up in an instant. "We don't need any help."

Carter snorted. "Get off your high horse. If there's a time to have somebody behind you in a battle, it's now."

"We don't have the money for that kind of battle," Hailey said. "And I can't help but think the Longfellows are behind these murders too."

"In what way?"

"In the way that makes my stomach churn."

"Because of Slim?" Gordon asked.

"Maybe. I just have a shitty feeling about it all."

"Well, with any luck, the sheriff does know what he's doing, and he will take care of things," Gordon said. "Carter, I know you feel very much like he doesn't care, but I think he does. Phil and Betty were good friends of his."

Hailey stopped and looked at him. "Yes, I forgot about that."

CHAPTER 5

T HE NEXT SEVERAL days passed in a blur. Hailey was sure
everybody was looking at her and muttering behind her
back. The company had been given access to their building,
and the business was carrying on, except it was just hellish
for her. She had triple sets of workloads to sort out, and
nothing was easy about any of it. Every partner had their
own system and was in charge of one-third of the employees,
and then every employee had their own way of doing things.
Fred and Phil had had systems that were not her way of
doing things. Two days later she looked up to find Carter
walking into her office. She glared at him.

He held up his hands. "I come in peace."

She shook her head. "With you, it's never that way."

"Why don't we bury the hatchet?" He sat in the visitor's
seat in her office. "Tell me if there's something I can do to
help."

Her instinctive answer was to order him out or to mock
his ability. But then she remembered his background in
finance and what Gordon had said earlier. "How much
finance do you remember?"

"I never got out of it," he said. "Even when I was in the
military, I was always involved in investments. But I'm still
not part of your world here. I don't exactly know what you
do, I guess."

"Investments," she said simply. "We handle various people's accounts. We're not accountants in terms of income tax, but we run a lot of books for people. But that's not our main focus. We handle the financial investments for several hundred companies."

"How big is your portfolio?"

She hesitated and then nodded. "Over $450 million."

His eyebrows shot toward his hairline, and he sagged back. "Wow. You guys have done well then."

"We've lost two companies since Fred and Phil were killed," she said, looking down at the paperwork on her desk. "I'm afraid a flood more are to follow."

"Did they say why?"

"One did because they've worked with Fred since forever and didn't trust anybody else. The other one didn't give an answer."

"You have to expect a certain amount of fallout after something like this. Trust is massive."

She nodded. "I need to sort out everything they were working on. Each of us has our own secretary, and I've got stacks of folders I'm supposed to be going through, alongside work in progress, so it's just a little too much."

"Did you even come home last night?"

"I did," she said, "but not until about eleven."

"Is there *anything* I can do to help you?"

"I don't know how or what. So much work is here that I don't know how to get somebody else to give me a hand." Her voice dropped when she said, "And I'm not sure who I can trust either."

Carter looked at the stacks of files behind her. "What if I took one of the partner's stacks? Whichever one is the most important, then I'll shuffle it in a priority list of what has to be done."

"Their secretaries tried to do that. I don't know how successfully exactly, but it's …" She trailed off. "The problem is, I probably need to bring in another junior partner or at least an assistant to help. I just don't know anybody I trust in my own business."

"And that's the bottom line again, right? So let me ask you this. Do you trust your brother?"

Her head bobbed. "Of course."

"Do you trust me?"

Instinctively she already knew the answer was a yes. "Yes, but you don't know these people or these accounts."

"So? You deal in finance, getting returns, regardless of the people who are your clients or the vehicles used to gain earnings." He turned and saw a small desk with a worn spot in the middle of its tabletop. She probably used to keep a printer there. "Why don't I sit here, while you give me a bunch of priority folders from one of the partners? Let me take a look."

She frowned, and he frowned right back. "I'd have to give you log-ins and such. Security is a big issue. I can't just give you carte blanche access."

"You'll have to give *someone* access," he said simply. "I'll take a laptop. Maybe one of the partners'?"

Hailey shook her head. "Both have been seized by the sheriff."

"Good. At least he's checking things like that. And he is bound to confidentiality, correct?"

"We locked out all access to the clients' files. I've shut down both partners' emails and locked them up so nobody can send to or from as well."

"Perfect," Carter said. "Put me in as a new person then.

As a consultant. With my own password to track my online work. Give me access to one partner's files." She hesitated, but he stared at her calmly. "You need help, and you need it now."

Frustrated, she opened her networking admin profile and gave him an account and an email, then set him up as a consultant. "This gives you limited access," she said. She glanced at a stack of files. "I've got five files of Phil's here. They were supposed to be next, but I just haven't gotten there yet."

"Not a problem," Carter said. He grabbed the stack and carried it back. "Let me take a look. Do we know what we're supposed to be looking for?"

"I printed off some of his emails and added them into each of the folders, so I had an idea of what the conversations were regarding the companies at the time."

"Great. Let me start reading those in the files."

Hailey pulled out one of her other laptops. She always kept a spare, multiples even. She opened it up, updated it, logged in with Carter's new email and set him up with a password. After that, she handed it to him and wrote down the password on a sticky note beside it. "I want you to keep using this one so I can track what you're doing."

"Good enough," he said. He was already distracted and quickly opened up the topmost company file.

Hailey watched him with her mouth open, wondering if she should ask him a question about his financial skills. After a while, she decided it was probably better to just leave him be. She didn't know what he knew, and this was a good way to find out. She needed help, no doubt about that. Nobody among the employees could move up to account manager. She had junior managers, but these were the senior accounts, and, because she had already found a problem earlier, she couldn't let anybody else in. And, if something here was connected to the murders, she didn't want anybody else to have access to that information either.

If Carter found something, that was a different story. Because, of all the people she knew, he was the one who could handle himself in the finance world. Even against a potential murderer. Gordon could handle the ranch just fine, and, when it came to a fistfight, would be the first one to throw a punch as needed, but, when it came to taking down an entire cavalry? She put her money on Carter. She dropped back in to study the massive work on her desk, until her phone rang.

She checked it and smiled. "Hey, Debbie. How are you doing?" She lifted her gaze and caught sight of Carter. She frowned at him, but he wasn't even looking at her.

"I heard you stopped in the other day, and I wasn't there," Debbie said.

"I stop in every once in a while, but you weren't there the last time, so I just carried on."

"Apparently somebody else stopped in to see me though, while I was out," Debbie said, her voice lightly probing. "Carter."

"Oh, did he?"

Hailey continued staring at Carter, but he still wasn't paying her any attention. "He's visiting the ranch for a few days, yes."

"Is he okay?" Debbie asked. "He took such a major hit that I was afraid he wouldn't pull through."

"He's actually in my office, giving me a hand right now."

"I heard about Fred," Debbie said. Her tone turned into

that of grief. "He was a very nice old man. I'm so sorry he thought he needed to take his own life."

Hailey scrunched up her face, hating to lie. "It's been tough around here. How are you doing?"

A strange hesitation came before Debbie answered. "Awful."

Hailey sagged in her chair. "In what way?"

"I miss the ranch. I miss you, and I miss Gordon."

"Can you find your way back?" Hailey asked gently, wanting to give her brother a swift boot for what he'd done. Debbie was a sweetheart.

"We have such a major problem," she said. "I don't know if I can go back to what we were, and I don't think he's ready to move forward."

Hailey could say nothing to that because it was the truth. Her brother was stuck in a lot of his old ways. "Just give him some time. I know he's miserable too."

"Is he?" Debbie asked hopefully. "That stupid man. I've loved him since forever."

"And you know the feeling's mutual."

"I know," Debbie said sadly. "But why is it that I can't live with somebody I love?" And just like that, she rang off.

Sad and torn, Hailey set her cell phone on the desk beside her. As she looked up this time, Carter studied her. She shrugged. "Debbie. She's miserable without Gordon, and Gordon's miserable without her."

Carter nodded. "I tried to get him to talk to her. I don't know if it did any good."

That surprised her. "You like Debbie, don't you?"

"More than that, I know Gordon's lost without her. They're really a perfect match. But sometimes your brother's a bit of a stick in the mud, and he doesn't see what he's got until he's lost it."

She smiled. "Exactly." She looked at the paperwork in front of her. She almost growled with frustration. "So many transactions are in just this one folder alone. I don't even understand how or why."

"If you're suspecting something underhanded and if it's over your head—and, no, I'm not saying it is—you can always get a forensic accounting audit done."

She looked up at him, startled. "What would that do?"

"They'll go back through the accounts to see if somebody has embezzled money or is running double books or cheating."

"Who do you know who does that?"

He settled back. "Me, for one."

She just stared at him.

"I kept my hand in investing, but I also started looking into company books as part of the military work I did. I found one problem when I was in one of my departments. I wasn't supposed to even have access to it. I went to one of the commanders, and, after that, I started working on other things and slowly did some private stuff for friends and companies. So, I was thinking about setting up something here like that."

"Titanium Corp," Hailey said. "Is that what you did for them?"

"No, but I could if they had that kind of work. I did carpentry and odd jobs for them. I thought I would set up a construction company and build houses." Carter grinned. "I do love the feel of a hammer in my hands, but delving into this kind of stuff and finding where people are trying to cheat is fascinating."

"Is that something you think you can handle?"

He eyed her steadily. "Do you think something's going on?"

She nodded and pulled out the two pieces of paper she had given copies of to the sheriff. She handed them to Carter. "I found these in the photocopier a few days before Fred was found dead."

He studied them carefully. "You know what companies these are from?"

"No. I've been trying to locate these particular ledgers. I have a search set up any time I open a file, but, so far, it hasn't pinged."

"When you find it, let me know," he said, "because this is bad news."

"I know. I wondered how much of it is related to the deaths."

"We can't discount it," he said, "because, as soon as you find embezzlement, you get fraud, then you get tax evasion, and you get people facing jail time. Things can get really ugly, really fast. That's the last thing we need."

"I know. I told the sheriff about it because I wanted to make sure he knew some problems existed in the company before the killings, and I was just starting to investigate."

"Good. It's always better to be honest about things like that."

"That's what I thought," she said, "but I'm still struggling."

"And now that I have an idea what we're looking for, more than normal trades and investments, I can help with that too. I wrote a couple programs that help me track entries across ledgers. I can set up something like that on this laptop."

CARTER WONDERED IF he should have offered his help. He wasn't a professional, but he had a knack for it. Still he wasn't a pro. He liked working with his hands and, therefore, took a great deal of pleasure in hammering and pounding and doing woodwork. But the challenge of the mental stimulation in doing this kind of work was something that was plain fun to him. The fact that a couple murders had already occurred and potentially something real nasty was going on even deeper added to the mystery.

That Hailey was involved was something much more dangerous yet again. Gordon would be destroyed if something happened to his sister. Carter wished he had come back a couple years ago now because maybe Gordon and Debbie wouldn't have broken up and maybe Hailey wouldn't be quite so embittered by whatever was going on.

As he had been worrying about healing himself, he hadn't thought about the impact and the positive effect he could have had on others. He had only seen the negatives— like how he would have required more assistance, how he would have been a burden, and how he couldn't have helped out as he normally would have at the ranch.

Now he remembered how well he and Debbie had gotten along and how he had helped to ease some of the difficulties she had had with Gordon even back then. If Gordon didn't get that message soon, he wouldn't have an opportunity to fix things with Debbie. She was a sweetheart, but she wanted one thing in her life, and that was a big family. Carter could well understand she'd leave Gordon to find somebody who could give her what she wanted. The desire for children shouldn't overtake a marriage, but he could see it happening in this case, what with Gordon's potential straying already fracturing the trust she had in her own husband.

Carter accessed some of his programs and downloaded one on this temporary laptop. It was a pretty simple software program, but it would show him how many times each of the entries had been changed and shifted. It would show keystrokes and multiple users alongside its history. He set it up to work and leaned back. Then, getting stiff, he stood and stretched his arms overhead. After that, he rotated his neck to loosen his shoulders. Hailey didn't even notice as he shifted.

She was busy chewing on her bottom lip, her gaze locked on her computer, and yet she typed with her left hand on the number keypad while she wrote with a pencil using her right hand. It was fascinating. Talk about a split-brain operation. This was multitasking to a whole new level. He didn't think he'd ever seen anybody do that before. He wanted to take a video of it but didn't want Hailey to think he was prying.

However, he knew, if he ever posted that on the internet, the world would go crazy. He brought out his phone and taped about thirty seconds of her working with both hands at the same time. He was careful not to show anything on the screen aside from the keyboard and the pad of paper, and nothing of her features either. Then he put it down and smiled.

"What were you just doing?" she asked. Her gaze didn't lift from the screen.

"I've never seen anybody type and write at the same time."

"If you want to keep track of stuff, you have to devise new and unique ways to do it. The world is a sucky place if you always do everything the same way."

He laughed. "Maybe, but I can't imagine doing what you're doing."

She glanced at her hands and smiled. "Not a biggie. I started a few years back. Actually, I think, when I was in college. I was always struggling to get caught up, and this seemed to be one of the few ways to do it."

"Good for you," he said. "I certainly can't."

She glanced over at his prosthetic. "And yet you're very good at computers."

"I learned to type fast with my right hand anyway. Never did learn to type properly, so this wasn't much of an issue."

"That was advance planning."

That startled a laugh out of him. Then he asked, "Do you have any idea who's been digging into the company and causing trouble?"

"I want to say it was Slim, but that's because I don't like him. Plus that's just way too easy as an answer. I don't think he has the computer skills to do this."

"Didn't take too much skill to leave photocopies in the Xerox machine."

"True, he was probably the idiot at the copier," she said. "But, as to this second-ledger business, if it *was* him, he's logged in as one of our three partners because I'm not seeing any other log-ins here."

"How hard would it be to get their log-ins?"

"Phil's, probably not too hard. He was lazy and wrote down everything on his desk. Fred was much more security-conscious."

"Places like this, security is everything," Carter said. He got an ill feeling when he thought about somebody being so cavalier about that. "The number of accounts someone could access through your company alone …"

"I hear you. It's one of the things I was fighting for before all this happened. Over this last year, Fred slowly came over to my way of thinking, but Phil wasn't even close."

"How often did that happen?"

"What happen?" She shook her head and tried to focus on him.

"How often did one partner side with you against the other partner?"

As if understanding this might be more serious than she initially thought, she sat back and frowned. "I'm not sure. Not very often. There hasn't been much we've disagreed on."

"Good. When there are three partners, it's always a bit of a worry.'

"If we had spent ten years together and had gone through multiple economic cycles especially, then maybe. But we have only been together for just over four years. As the youngest member, I was always much more deferential to their wishes. But I have been finding my voice lately," she admitted. "And a few things—like the physical and the online security—I was getting to be a big stickler on."

"Do you have an IT company that handles it?"

"We do. They're very good." She named a company he'd heard of. "Of course that's no guarantee they don't have a problem within their own system, but we didn't see anything."

"Well, Phil obviously left his log-in information lying around," Carter said. "So then it'd be easy enough for somebody else to get it, whether a client in for a face-to-face visit or an employee. Particularly if they knew that's what he did. So we need to focus on Phil's folders first."

"Yes. And one of the people I need to talk to is his secretary."

"Oh, that's a good idea. Does she have any boyfriends within the company?"

A glimmer of a smile whispered across her face. "Not a boyfriend but a husband who is friends with Slim. His name is Andy. The two have been best friends forever. Andy might even be related to the Longfellows too. I don't know. And that was exactly what I was thinking of."

CHAPTER 6

HAILEY WASN'T SURE if she should be bothered or grateful that Carter was on the same wavelength she was. She motioned at the computers in front of her. "Somebody must have had access and had to know what they were doing."

"What does her husband do for the company?"

"Andy is a junior analyst."

"So, potentially he knows enough to get into trouble?"

"Potentially. He also has a connection to get the log-ins from her."

"We need them interviewed again, from this embezzlement angle. Any chance you can get the sheriff to do it, so you're kept out of it?"

"I was thinking about stopping by his office today," she said slowly. "I don't want to cause trouble where there isn't any, but we do need to get to the bottom of this."

"I'll come with you," he said. Then he motioned toward the laptop. "How secure is this room?"

She glanced at the locked door. "I guess if somebody has the keys, it's not that secure."

"The door has a keypad for a passcode on top of the doorknob."

"Yes, but we stopped using that and went back to the keyed entry. Everybody kept getting the codes wrong." She watched his eyebrows go up and shrugged. "As I said, I'm trying to get certain things fixed."

"Do you know if you can go back to using the passcode? We'll lock it with a key but also with the passcode, if possible."

"I can for my office," she said. "I don't know about Phil's though."

"Puts Phil back to being the weakest link again."

Hailey watched Carter's face as he turned to the door. It was almost like she could see the wheels spinning behind that gaze. She had forgotten how intelligent he was. The last couple times she'd seen him, they'd done nothing but fight. She saw a different side to him now. Maybe that was just her letting him in because she needed his help.

"Possibly," she said, "but we can't look at that just because it's an easy assumption."

He chuckled. "I would say something similar. Can we get into Phil's office?"

She nodded and stood. "Come on. I'll take you." She locked her office and walked over to Phil's. She would have unlocked the door with her key, but it was already unlocked when she twisted the knob. She swore under her breath. "That should never have happened."

"Unless the sheriff's department has taken all electronics, and nothing is left?"

"I know. But I would still say that nobody should have left these rooms unlocked."

Carter wandered through Phil's office that offered a good view. "Will you take a corner office now?"

She shrugged. "I'm not sure what I'll do actually. It's a very strange position to be in."

"Just try to get through this rough weather and see what

it looks like on the other side of the storm."

"Depends on how long this storm goes on," she said. "Something like this is more damaging if it never gets solved. If it does get resolved, at least we have answers, whether I like them or not."

"And rumors are deadly in the financial world. Did the sheriff take Phil's laptop?"

"I'll confirm that. You're definitely right—that's one of the big things." She pulled out her phone and called the sheriff. "The door was also unlocked when I opened it up just now. It was locked, and I did lock it again when I was here this morning."

The sheriff sucked in his breath. "So, you're saying somebody went into that room and left it unlocked? Did they take anything?"

"Not that I can see," she said. "I'll run through the security feeds for the building. I'll get back to you." With that, she hung up.

"Why didn't you mention the security feeds earlier?" Carter asked.

She sighed. "Maybe because I just learned both my partners are dead. I'm not thinking straight—not to mention the fact that the sheriff was already talking about our video feeds. So I assumed he was looking at them."

"Where are they?"

Hailey led the way downstairs to one of the back rooms. She sensed the odd looks Carter was getting from other people. The company was now hers, and she appeared to be on chummy terms with him. They didn't know who he was—he was a stranger in a place like this—and that was the worst thing one could be here in a town full of Longfellows. Hailey sighed.

Meanwhile, Carter ignored them all and followed her into a small room full of feeds and security camera equipment. "Where do you have the cameras?" he asked.

"One is at the top of the stairs, but it's been disabled."

"Since when?"

"Since May," she said bluntly. "At a May Day party that crossed the line a bit."

He just stared at her.

"Yes. I know. Apparently a couple people tried to take advantage of one of the upstairs offices for a private room. Somebody disabled the camera but did such a good job that we're supposed to be getting a new one but haven't yet."

"It's July."

"I know. We haven't had it fixed. Again, one more thing I argued about."

"What is to even argue about? It should have just been done."

"I put through the vouchers to get it done," she said. "And our business accountant went to Fred for approval, and Fred brought it to me, then he brought it to Phil, and they both thought it was a waste of time and money. But I said, if it was good money to put it in, in the first place, it was good money to fix it, but the old men were stubborn."

She watched as Carter stared at her uncomprehendingly.

"Small town. And you have to understand they didn't think anything bad would ever happen."

"But you did?"

"I didn't like Slim," she said bluntly. "Didn't trust a damn thing about him. And when you don't trust somebody, you always look around and wonder just what all else could be going on."

"Okay, so we don't have any cameras on the top floor.

What about on the stairwells and the elevators?"

"Stairwells, yes. Elevators, no."

He brought up the stairwell feed. "Do you have a company that looks after this security?"

"Yes, but they just handle maintenance on the equipment."

"But not enough maintenance to put the camera on the top floor back up and running, it seems."

"No, in fact, one of the maintenance guys got involved at the May Day party with one of the married secretaries. That's how he knew which camera to disable."

"For God's sake."

"Right?" Hailey laughed. "So, I'll give you his name too. If you want to tear him apart, that would be just fine because he certainly isn't planning on listening to me."

"Why is that?"

"He's a Longfellow."

"DOES EVERYTHING COME back to the Longfellows?"

"They're like a virus," Hailey said. Her voice held a certain mirth but with no laughs. "You'll find them everywhere. Very contagious. You can catch the virus just by brushing past them."

"So, let me get this straight. That Longfellow is one of your IT guys, and he was here for a May Day party where he knew there was a camera, then disabled it, so he could have a tryst with somebody from the company. Correct?"

"Correct, and the secretary was *married*." She emphasized the last word.

"Good God," he said. "This is worse than a soap opera."

"It *is* a soap opera," she said. "Anyway, the sheriff knows about the security issue, and he knows the company handling our security, but he also knows our IT guy is a Longfellow, also related to Fred. So, if we find anything, that's one thing. But, if we have to go to that Longfellow to get it, that's a different story, and security and privacy will then be an issue."

"It shouldn't be," he said. "They should be locked down to secrecy at this point."

"Well, again, this is a small town, and everybody knows everybody."

"I don't care if he's married to you. He shouldn't be telling anybody what the hell's going on."

"In theory, he shouldn't be," she said. "But in reality …"

Carter shook his head and kept going through the feed. "So, we can't see the top floor. We can't see the elevator, and I'm not seeing anything in the stairs. I presume everybody in the company knows the camera on the top floor isn't working and none are in the elevators?"

"I don't know for sure, but I'll take a stab and say yes. And, if they had all known, and they have all spoken about it, then chances are three-quarters of the town knows too."

He flicked through the cameras. "And yet this one is running."

She leaned forward. "Yeah, I'm the one who insisted on that one going up. But they never connected it to the main system because they thought I was being foolish."

"A security camera in a parking lot is being foolish?"

"'Money out the window' is what Fred would have said."

"Wow." Carter whistled. "They sound like backward hicks, and yet they're involved in finance and investments."

"Exactly. We have more firewalls and safeguards on our

company's internet databases than we do on actual physical security."

"What use is any of that digital security if Phil wrote down his log-ins?" Carter asked.

"You're asking the wrong person. Like I told you before, I'm the one who fought the lack of online security. I can only do so much with two older guys from another generation."

"Wrong," he corrected. "There's only so much you *could* do. That's all about to change."

She looked at him and smiled. "I guess the first thing I should do is see if I can find a competing company for security without any Longfellow involvement. Then I'll change how the passwords are dealt with."

"I would get somebody not even close to this city. Surely somebody bigger handles stuff out this far too."

"Maybe. I'll check into that."

"I'd check into it fast because you don't know what all else they might be accessing."

"What do you mean?" Hailey asked.

"For instance, what if they have hidden cameras in your office and can check your log-in as you type it in? It's not that far out of the realm of possibility." He watched the color fade from her skin.

She wrapped her arms around her chest.

He walked over and said, "I'm not trying to scare you ..."

She shook her head. "No, it's not that. I just always had the feeling my office was being watched."

He froze and then put a finger to his lips. He pulled her close and whispered, "We'll search the offices for bugs and cameras."

"But I don't know how," she said.

He stepped away and said, "It's probably just your imagination. I see nothing suspicious in this security office. Let's go back to work."

They locked the door behind them, and Hailey made a point of locking the keypad too.

Carter nodded in agreement. However, when they reached the hallway, Carter looked around and whispered, "We need to get some equipment."

"Sure, but, while we don't have it yet, I have work to do," Hailey said, as they returned to her office.

"Can you work from home today?"

She frowned but nodded.

He motioned for her to pack up everything, and he grabbed all of what he had been working on. He stopped when he looked at the folders and told her maybe they should take them all home.

"Pardon?" she asked in confusion. He motioned to the files spread about her office.

She grabbed a box and stacked the files, then put in her laptop, leaving the one he'd been using.

"I'll take that to my truck," Carter told her after she finished packing.

"Okay," she said. They stepped out, and she locked not only the knob but also the keypad.

After that, they went to Fred's office. Nothing was left to lock up, as the sheriff had taken it all. She led the way down the back staircase and out into the parking lot, where Carter put the box in Gordon's borrowed truck while Hailey got in her truck. When she was inside her vehicle, Carter walked over to her side and leaned in.

"I want you to go straight home," he said. "I'll make a

couple phone calls and get a shipment of tracking equipment sent to me." She frowned at him, and he shook his head. "No arguing. We need to know if there's a video problem."

"We already know there's a problem. What we need to know is how extensive it is."

"I can get something in overnight. Or I can take the afternoon and make a trip to pick up the closest equipment. I've got to think about that."

"Fine," she said, "but I have to go grocery shopping before I go home."

"Okay. You do that. Just be careful, will you?"

She nodded and backed up and out of the parking lot. After that, Carter hopped into his truck and headed out too. He didn't go too far. He went up and around the corner, pulled onto the shoulder, and called Geir to explain what the problem was.

Geir stopped him midway. "Okay, so a hell of a lot is going on there with your friends, but what about the dog?"

"Longfellows dropped the ball on the dog," Carter answered. "Get me some tracking equipment. I know it's all connected. I just don't know how."

"You better find that dog though," Geir warned.

"I will," he said, ending the call. His fingers tapped a staccato on the wheel as he thought about it. Then he contacted Brenda's driver.

"Hey, it's Carter again," he said.

The driver was almost sullen.

"I need the dog."

A shocked silence came on the other end before the old man spoke. "I don't have the dog."

"You don't, but I need to know what you did with him." And again more silence followed. "Look. I don't care what problems you have or how much trouble you might have gotten into with this dog. I think you let the dog loose somewhere. Probably for its own sake, but I need to know where, so I can find it."

The driver spoke a spot of Spanish and then suddenly he said, "I let it go just outside the airport."

"How long ago?"

"On the day it arrived. It was sitting there, waiting to be picked up, and I didn't want to pick it up because I knew what Brenda would be like to the dog," the old man said in a rush. "Nobody was around, so I opened up the cage and got the dog outside. Then the dog just took off. I don't think he appreciated sitting in the cage all that time either. Maybe he knew what freedom was."

"So now we have a lost dog. Have you seen it since?"

"No, I haven't. Now leave me alone."

The driver hung up before Carter could respond. Carter called Geir again and told him the news.

"Wow, Brenda's so bad to animals that her driver thought the dog would be better off on its own?" Geir asked.

"I'm not so sure I trust that statement either, but I do think he did something with the dog so it wouldn't be with Brenda."

"You think he took it?"

"I don't know," Carter said. "I need his and his granddaughter's addresses."

"Ah. Well, give me some names, and I'll see what I can find."

By the time Carter hung up, he felt better. What he really wanted to know was where the granddaughter was and what were the chances that she had a dog named Matzuka. With nothing better to do now, he headed back to the ranch.

As he turned the engine on, however, two vehicles came ripping up the road. Both had been parked at this trucking company lot while he'd been here on the phone. He'd seen them. He didn't know who they were, but, at the speed they were going, they were on a mission. He pulled up behind them, driven by curiosity. He decided he would follow them and see just where they went.

CHAPTER 7

A FTER CUTTING SHORT her grocery shopping, getting only what she needed for tonight and tomorrow, Hailey drove home, her mind buzzed with confusion and odd thoughts. She hated to say it, but it felt like fear. She was afraid somebody was deliberately trying to sabotage her company. Afraid that more than trying to sabotage the business, the perpetrator had killed her partners and was after her now.

She couldn't stop herself from looking in the rearview mirror to see if she was being followed. The road was clear, but she wished Carter had come behind her. She chastised herself for that thought. That was foolish. She didn't want to be dependent on him. The fact that he had stepped up to help review the files was already huge. It also marked a turning point in their relationship. It was hard to be angry at somebody deliberately trying to help you out.

Maybe he had always been like that. Maybe she simply didn't know because she'd only seen the mockery and the joking. He had almost a hard edge to him now. And maybe she just wanted to see it that way so she could back away from her emotions—away from the disappointment and the pain.

She couldn't believe it when he'd married that bitch. At that time, Hailey had been hurt and distraught. Finally he had woken to the truth about his wife and now acted like a completely different person—and, well, so was she. She didn't want to say maybe this was a second chance for them, but she couldn't help thinking it. So many good things could come out of this, and yet, at the same time, it was kind of hard to go there. After all, she had spent years staying away from him and deliberately being mean and caustic to keep him back. But now he was divorced with a new start in life. And here she was with a new start too, whether she had asked for it or not …

She wanted to be joyful that the company was hers, but to think it came on the blood of her partners was not a happy thought. She had always preferred to scale her own mountains and to achieve her own success. This felt like a backhanded win. It wasn't what she'd wanted at all. At one point, she had dreamed about buying out her partners and having the company all to herself—but not this way. Never this way.

She took a few more corners heading toward home when she realized two vehicles were coming up very quickly behind her. She automatically slowed down.

She was driving a good reliable and heavy truck, never taking a chance on a poor choice of wheels while living out on the ranch. One of the vehicles drove past and sent a cloud of dust into her face. She let out a breath of relief, thinking the driver must be in a hurry. But then he pulled in front of her and slowed down. Not sure what that meant, she slowed down ever-so-slightly. Then the realization hit her. The second vehicle was still behind her. That did not make her happy.

Instead of letting these two vehicles dictate her actions, she swiftly drove around the one in front of her and gunned it to get past him. The driver was caught unaware by her move, and she managed to zip in front. As she drove by, she caught the surprise on his face and realized it was someone who worked for her.

What the hell was going on? She kept driving, keeping her eyes ahead. She wasn't sure if that was a deliberate pincer maneuver or if something else was going on here, and she had misunderstood their urgency. She hesitated and wondered if she should pull over and wait until they pulled up again. But then again she wasn't sure. After what had happened to her partners, she didn't dare take the chance.

Then she saw a third vehicle come closer. She frowned. She was heading toward her ranch now. Were the other three heading there too? Taking a chance, once again, she maxed out her foot pedal on the gas and whipped farther ahead. Then she hit the brake to surprise them and took the turn as fast as she could, so she was the only one heading down her driveway and waited to see what would happen. The other vehicles passed her through the cloud of dust. She caught a faint glimpse of the second driver, but it was enough to make an ID. The last vehicle, which appeared to be Carter, turned down the drive behind her.

When she got to the front of the house, she parked and hopped out, her hands shaking. She waited for Carter.

"Are you okay?" he asked.

"Was that weird, or was something going on there?" Her voice broke. "What the hell was that?"

"It looked like a special maneuver. Do you know those two men?"

"They both work for the company, or rather Slim used to and Andy still does," she said in shock. "I need to contact the sheriff."

"Good," he said. "I'm trying to figure out what to do about that damn dog too."

She stared at him. "Right. That's the reason you're here."

"Do you know Brenda Longfellow's driver?"

She frowned. "Diego?"

He nodded. "Must be. He told me that he let the dog go out into the wild."

She shook her head. "I can't see him doing that. He loves animals. He used to run a center for injured animals. He'd care for them."

"Ah," Carter said. "You know where his granddaughter lives?"

"Because of what the Burgess kid did or because of the dog?"

"How about both?" he said with a half smile. "Do you want to come with me in order to smooth things over? If she's got the dog, then you can bet everything is okay."

"Maybe, but is it possible to find the dog and remove it? Is that what you want to do?"

He frowned. "I just need to know if the dog is okay. I don't have to take personal responsibility for it."

"Why don't we go out and take a look then?" Hailey asked.

"Right. I should have done that first. Right at the beginning, I was afraid that's what he had done."

"Why would you think that?"

"Just something about the way he reacted," Carter said, leaning into the truck and pulling out the office box with her laptop. He walked inside and placed the box down on the counter, then turned and nudged her back outside. At the truck he motioned at the passenger side. "Let's go talk to her."

"We should have told my brother what I was doing," Hailey said after a while.

"He's probably out with the cows," Carter said with a laugh.

"As long as he's okay."

Carter's brows furrowed. "Do you think somebody'll hurt him?"

"Not necessarily," she said. "But I just know this war is heating up on all sides."

"So, do you think the property war is related to your partners?"

She raised both hands, shaking her head. "I have no idea. None of this makes any sense. I would never have thought Fred or Phil could be involved in something like that. But the rest of their families—who knows—maybe."

"It will make sense. Eventually. We just don't have all the pieces."

While he drove, following her instructions, Hailey called the sheriff. She told Raleigh what had just happened with the two vehicles. Then she glanced at Carter. "I should have put that call on Speaker."

"Doesn't matter," he said. "What did he have to say?"

"He said he's made a note of it, and they have Phil's laptop. He also said he did check the security cameras but didn't find or see anything."

"Okay."

"I guess that's what I expected."

"We didn't really see anything either, except I did see one vehicle entering the parking lot, then leaving soon afterward early that Monday morning when you found Fred's body," Carter said. "So maybe somebody knew about the camera in the parking lot and used that knowledge to avoid being seen."

"What vehicle was it?"

"Fred's, per a license plate check."

"So after Fred was killed, they left from Phil's window, explaining why that was left open. Adding weight to the fact that Phil probably killed him."

"At least that's what somebody wants to make it look like," Carter said with a frown.

"I don't know who would want to smear his name like that. Phil's always been well loved."

"But apparently he was a slacker in the IT arena."

"Yes, but that doesn't necessarily mean anything. People who are often very popular, it's their very popularity that lets them get away with doing less than others."

"They might get away with more shit," he agreed, "but that doesn't mean they get respect that way."

"Possibly. It's really hard to know."

"Exactly."

She directed Carter around a couple corners to the back part of town, where many small hobby farms were. They looked run-down.

"He lives in here," Hailey said.

"The granddaughter?"

"The whole family lives together. You don't really think Brenda pays enough for them to have separate houses, do you?"

CARTER FROWNED AT that but stayed quiet. They went around two more corners that opened up to a small and clean but older home, with a lot of dogs running in kennels. Carter pulled into the driveway and hopped out. Instead of heading to the main house with Hailey, he went to the dog kennels. He didn't find Matzuka. Frowning, he turned around to see Brenda's driver standing nearby.

Carter put his hands on his hips. "I'm looking for the dog, and I won't stop until I find him."

Diego shook his head. "I don't have him."

"Why?"

The man hesitated.

Just then Hailey appeared. "Hi, Diego, how are you doing?"

His face broke into a smile. He reached out and shook her hand. "I'm doing fine." Then he looked at Carter and frowned. "Tell him that I don't have the dog."

"If you don't have the dog, then you know where it is," she said gently.

Diego looked distressed at that.

When Hailey saw that, she added, "It's a well-known fact you'd never hurt an animal, and neither would you release one to the wild, alone and lost, with the possibility to get in trouble."

His gaze turned sad.

"I don't know why you think you're in trouble. We just want the dog." He shrugged but stayed silent, and she pressed a little harder. "You do understand the US government's after it, right?"

"I do."

"Then please be truthful and just tell us. We won't tell Brenda," Carter said.

Diego snorted. "That's what you say. That doesn't mean it won't get back to her."

"Did you open the cage?"

Diego hesitated.

"So, you didn't," Carter said. "Did you see somebody else open the cage?"

At that, he looked distressed again.

"Is the dog loose and running free somewhere?" Carter pushed.

Diego shrugged. "I haven't seen him."

"Have you tried?"

He nodded. "I have tried, but I haven't seen him."

"When I first arrived," Carter said, "I thought I saw a coyote along the back of the airport. Matzuka looks like a coyote. His colors are very much fawn colors. He's been missing for three months. That's a long time."

"Plus lots of garbage can be found around the airport," Diego said. "Sometimes dogs can survive there without problems."

"You didn't open the cage, and you didn't see the dog, but you know something about him. What happened?"

The driver's shoulders slowly sagged. "I wasn't there. I told you about my granddaughter." He glanced from Carter to Hailey. They both nodded. "But my nephew, ... he works there sometimes. He thought the dog looked sad. My nephew's special."

At that, Hailey remembered his nephew had Down's syndrome. She nodded. "Did he let the dog out because the dog looked sad? Did he want to play with the dog for a little bit?"

Diego brightened. "You remember him?"

"Of course I do. Carlos is a very happy boy." Hailey thought he was about twelve now, physically, but she didn't really know what age he was mentally.

"He goes to the airport with his father, where he washes cars in the parking lot for money."

"And Carlos was on his own when he saw the dog and opened the cage? He let the dog out, hoping to play with him but lost him?" Hailey asked. She talked with gentleness and empathy.

Diego nodded and sighed heavily. "I've been looking for the dog, but I've seen no sign of him."

"The airport is not very close to you," Carter said. "Have you been driving by to check out the neighborhood?"

"I drive by," the old man said. "I always have dog food, and I leave some at the airport, hoping I can capture him again."

"Because you knew someone would be checking in on this dog, didn't you?"

"Whenever the government's involved, yes," he said. "The minute I understood it was a War Dog, I knew we would be in trouble." Then he raised his hands, palms showing, and took a deep breath before continuing, "But what can I do? I wasn't there with Carlos. He was there alone for a bit—only because his mom was at work, while his dad was trying to get work in the parking lot at the airport. Then Carlos wandered off for a few minutes. He saw the dog, and I was late, so I should have had the dog, but I didn't, and Carlos let him go."

Hailey smiled. "You know what? It isn't the end of the world. We just need to find the dog now."

"But what can I do? I've never seen the dog."

"Not at all?"

"Once, maybe twice," he said. "Only in the first week."

"Okay," Carter said. "I'll go to the airport area and see if I can track it. It's unfortunately been a little too long for me to track anything fresh. Where did you last see him?"

"About an hour away from the airport or about a couple miles from there, near a small dump pile everybody just throws crap into. So often food is there, which leads to a problem with the bears sometimes too, but always coyotes are there."

"Matzuka would handle coyotes just fine," Carter said, "but it's still not an ideal lifestyle, is it?"

Diego shook his head. "No, I should have told you in the first place."

"Yes, you should have."

"Let's go take a look now," Hailey said.

"Yeah," Carter replied. "I'm worried somebody else has picked him up."

"Maybe," Diego said suddenly. "I think I saw somebody with a shepherd like that in town the other day."

"Who was it?"

"Harold," he said. "Harold Longfellow."

"*Another* Longfellow?" Carter shook his head as he glanced at Hailey before turning toward Diego.

He nodded. "One of the nastier ones."

"Oh, crap," Hailey said. "Slim's cousin. Yeah, I can see him wanting a shepherd like that."

"Was he treating him well?" Carter asked.

"The dog wasn't behaving, and he was a little rough with it," Diego said. "But you dare not criticize or comment on the Longfellows' behavior."

"He wasn't using the dog to threaten anybody, was he?"

"The dog wore a big collar with spikes on it. Harold is bad news. I think he runs a bookie operation and also loans money to the down-and-out locals in this town." He flashed a look at Carter. "His interest rates basically mean he's bought many an indentured servant."

At that, Carter looked at Hailey.

"I don't know about any of that," she said. "I just know, back when we were in school, he used to be the punk at the street corner, maybe doing marijuana sales. So he's got ties into that drug culture from way back then. He wasn't into the bigger drugs or anything, not that I heard, but he may have upscaled to the betting and loans hustle instead. It would go along with his street image. He wears a vest and has a lot of tattoos. But still, in their case, family's family."

"And, of course, the dog was supposed to go to Brenda and David, but they don't know anything about where it ended up, right? And, if they did find out, after the fact, would they have said anything?" Carter asked Hailey.

"Maybe. But Brenda doesn't like Harold. Brenda is probably the only one in the entire family who would not have given him the dog. Although, if Harold threatened her, she might bend."

Diego nodded. "I think that's what happened. But I can't be sure."

"How can I find this guy?"

Hailey sucked in her breath and shook her head. "You don't want to do that."

"Why not?"

She frowned. "Because I don't care how tough you think you are, Harold's generation is just mean."

"It doesn't sound like they're very nice at *any* generation," he said. "Besides, I just want to know that the dog is safe and sound. If he's not happy there, I will find him a place where he is happy."

"We could take him together," Diego said brightly.

Carter smiled. "I'll take that into consideration, but it

could jeopardize your job with Brenda."

"I need another job. But it's hard to get another job because I won't get any references from her."

"Can't stand that kind of crap. Look. If I come up with another job for you, I'll let you know." Carter waved at him, then motioned Hailey back to the truck.

"Do you believe him?" Carter asked Hailey after he turned on the engine.

"I don't know what I believe anymore," she said. "It seems like a whole pile of slithering snakes is beneath my feet that I didn't see before. My ability to judge is severely skewed now."

"I hear you. Can't say I'm too thrilled about it myself."

"What will you do about the dog?"

"I'd love to take him by force," he said, then sighed. "I really don't know the extent of my authority. It's official navy business, yet it's not. I'll talk to Geir about that, I guess."

As if on cue, his phone rang. He looked at it and smiled. "It's Geir," he said. He reversed the vehicle and headed down the road as he answered it, putting the call on speaker phone while he was driving. "Geir, what's up?"

"A parcel's coming for you. Overnight delivery. You can pick it up at the post office today."

"Will do. I also have heard that the dog was let loose at the airport," Carter said, telling him what he'd learned.

"So," Geir said, "the third time around, do you think you're actually getting the right story?"

"I think the driver cares a lot about his family, and I think he was protecting his nephew," Carter said. "The question is whether the dog is any better off where he is now."

"Well, we can't just assume. We need to make sure he's not being abused."

"I plan on heading into known drug territory. Apparently Harold is also a Longfellow. From the wrong side of the tracks though. Not well-loved by the rest of the family and part of a street hustle."

"Right. Of course. And he's looking for a big macho sidekick of a War Dog to make him feel like an even bigger man, I suppose?"

"I think so," Carter said. "From what I'm hearing, that would fit. The thing is, according to Hailey, he's dangerous."

"Yeah, well, we know what that's all about," Geir said, sounding tired. "Wouldn't it be nice if we actually had good guys involved for a change? And why can't these dogs ever end up with somebody who's busy making sunshine and smelling roses or something?"

"Yeah, that doesn't seem to be the way of it," Carter said.

"Maybe not, but it's certainly something that would be nice to have as a change around here."

"Anyway, I'll have to check up on this new location and see if I can get a hold of him. Then we'll see if we can come up with a solution."

"Are you planning on just walking up to him and asking for the dog back?" Geir asked.

"You can bet he'll ask for proof of ownership," Carter said.

"You've got it all in the file. The adoption forms, his chart, and the other documents in his file—not to mention the tattoos. Maybe you should ask him for *his* proof of ownership."

"Yeah." Carter laughed. "It'll be behind a nine millimeter. You know that."

"You've been there before," Geir said with amusement, "but it would be a good idea if you didn't go alone."

"Maybe, but backup isn't something I have available."

"Of course," Geir answered, "because that would just be way too easy. Since you've already shared how the local law enforcement is infested with Longfellows, I'll have to look farther out. I'll get back to you when I come up with something else here. In the meantime, do some more fieldwork, but don't take too much action if it'll lead to trouble with the local authorities."

"Gotcha," Carter said before he hung up. He tossed the phone down beside him. "Do you know where this guy lives?" he asked Hailey.

"No, but anybody in the slums could tell you," she said quietly.

"Direct me to that area so I can take a look at what I'm up against."

She gave him the directions, heading back around town.

"What is the population count there?"

"About thirty thousand," she said. "But that includes all the ranches surrounding the area too, for quite a few miles."

"Right. So, the core of the town is what, twenty, maybe twenty-five thousand?"

"Less. Maybe half that. It's big enough to have schools and a sheriff and several deputies but not necessarily large enough to have big box stores or anything else like that."

"Of course not. You have to drive what? An hour and a half to get that kind of shopping and dining?"

"Yes," she said. She motioned up ahead. "Turn here."

He made the left turn, and she directed him around two more corners.

"Now you should recognize the area," she said.

"When pawnshops start showing up," he said, "it usually gives me the best indication that I'm in the right area."

"I'm not sure if Harold stands on street corners himself now, but he has a lot of his minions who would likely be doing the deals on the corners."

"But he's not too high up in the street system, is he?"

"I don't know," she said. "I used to go to school with him, but he's not the man I used to know. Oh, stop! I think that's him right there."

Carter pulled off to the side of the road and watched as a big tattoo-covered male walked down the street. A shepherd was at his side with a studded collar on it. Carter looked at the collar with disgust, then checked out the dog more closely, and reached for the files on his phone. Once he found the photo, he held it up. He pointed it at Hailey. "What do you think?"

She nodded. "That looks like the dog."

Carter hopped out of the truck and darted through the traffic to approach Harold. The guy looked at him and raised an eyebrow. "Dude, what can we do for you?"

Instead of answering, Carter made a sharp whistle and gave a couple hand commands. Immediately the dog's head and ears went up as it sat down and then lay down, pulling the leash farther away from Harold's hand.

Harold jerked the leash hard. "What the fuck did you just do to my dog?"

"Well," Carter said with a smile, "he answered a couple questions for me." He reached down and ordered the dog to stretch out. Carter took a look at the inside of its leg. "I'll be reclaiming Uncle Sam's property now." With a sudden and swift move, he disconnected the dog's collar and let it drop, releasing the dog.

The man swore at Carter and chased the dog, trying to hook him back up. "What the fuck did you do that for?"

"That dog was shipped here specifically for an adoptive family. It was accidentally freed. I'd like to know how you have US Navy property in your possession."

"Yeah, well, I've been good to him. Giving him food and all kinds of good treatment."

"Except for the fact that it's not your dog," Carter said. "It's a War Dog. I'll be taking him back with me." He called the dog to him, and it came like lightning. He bent down and gave his head the cuddle and the chin scratches he probably missed. The dog was overjoyed because now somebody spoke his language. Then, without giving the other guy a chance, Carter walked to Gordon's truck, opened the door, and ordered the dog up.

"Thanks for looking after my dog for me," Carter said before he hopped in and drove off.

CHAPTER 8

H AILEY STARED AT Carter. "I'm not sure you should have done that," she said, twisting so she could look out the rearview window.

"Maybe not," he said. "But enough shit is going on here that we need to figure out how it all is related. I wanted to take the dog out of the equation. Plus you gotta stand up to bullies." Matzuka sat behind him, head forward, almost between the two of them. "How are you, boy?"

He gave a light bark, seemingly perfectly happy.

"You took the leash off. Don't you need the collar for him?"

"Not if he's a properly trained K9," he said. "Their training is crazy."

"How did you know those commands?"

"I used to work with dogs. We raised dogs too in my family growing up and my ex-wife and I had two dogs, both of which she took when she left. But, when I knew I was coming here, I contacted a friend of mine and learned some more commands that Matzuka would be used to. One of the biggest things my friend said was that my commands had to be issued with absolutely no hesitation. *Make sure you give the command with the expectation of being obeyed because, as soon as the dog hears any doubt in the command, he takes advantage of it.* In this case, these dogs should know better than that. But Matzuka hasn't been around the K9 unit for a very long time now."

"Did you double-check the tattoo?"

"Yes," he said. "Didn't you see me order him to lie down? I checked his tattoo then."

"So, what now? You'll have multiple Longfellows after you."

"Harold is the one they don't like, so chances are the others will just laugh at him, and that'll make him even angrier. If he knew the dog was meant for Brenda to begin with, that would explain why he took it. But chances are good he just found the dog without knowing or checking on its history."

"And what about Brenda? Doesn't she get rights back to the dog?"

"No, she signed off on official US Navy papers, saying she never received Matzuka, which means she has no liability for or responsibility to the dog."

"He currently doesn't have an owner then," Hailey said curiously.

"Sure, he does," Carter said with a big grin. "Me."

She shook her head. "Wow."

"*Wow* what?"

"When you move, you move fast," she said. She settled into the passenger seat and turned to look at the dog, a shepherd, although slightly bigger. Its tongue lolled out to the side. "So, do you think he'll be happy? What if he bonded with Harold?"

"I doubt it," Carter said. "Did you see how he was pulling on him?"

"Oh, no," she said in a deadly voice, "his shoulders and back have welts."

He shot her a hard glance, studying the dog closer but keeping an eye on the road too.

"You probably didn't get a chance to notice earlier," she said, "but it looks like he's been beaten with a belt or something."

"All the more reason to make sure Harold loses him permanently."

"Are you expecting him to come after the dog?"

"No, but that doesn't mean he won't. It also depends on whether he saw you or not."

She sighed. "It's possible. I mean, I've spent my lifetime here, and I went to school with him." Just then her phone rang. *Unknown caller.* "Hello?" she said cautiously.

Harold's voice blasted through the truck. "Give my fucking dog back, bitch!" And he hung up.

She stared at the phone in fascination. "Well, I guess he does remember who I am."

"Good," Carter said. "Do you have his caller number there?"

She held it up and nodded.

"Hit Dial and hand me the phone."

Hailey sighed but did what Carter asked. She didn't want to get caught up in any more Longfellow disputes.

As soon as the angry voice answered on the other end, Carter said, "This dog belongs to a department of the US military defense system. I verified its War Dog tattoo, and you have obviously beaten this very expensive animal. Charges will be pending." And, with that, he hung up. He tossed the phone back to Hailey.

Shocked, she wasn't sure what to think. "*Are* charges pending?"

"Maybe. Probably not though. Nobody ever seems to

give a shit about animal abuse, which pisses me off. But, if Harold causes any trouble, you can bet I'll bring down his little street operation."

"You really think you can?"

"I can. The problem is, as soon as I do, ten more heads will pop out of the shadows to take over for him."

"But still," she said, "I've heard he's gotten a lot worse lately."

"Worse in what way?"

"Just the way he's treating people on the streets. He does have the same blood as the idiot student who beat up Diego's granddaughter."

"You have enough things to worry about," Carter said. "You let me worry about this one. As soon as we get to your house, we'll take a look at the dog and see if he needs medical treatment. I don't know if you can trust a vet around here who's not a Longfellow though."

Hailey brightened up. "There is one. She's relatively new to the area and bought out a practice the Longfellows didn't like."

"Did they run the old vet out of business?"

"More or less. I already told you how crossing them is never a good idea."

"Then I have doubts about the new vet not already being tainted if the Longfellows allowed her to take over the practice." Carter shook his head. "Sounds like a real shake-up is needed in this area. The Longfellows are out of control. Somebody has to stand up to them."

"Maybe," she said. And then she sank back in her seat. "I just don't know who'll make that happen."

She closed her eyes and wished she could go back in time a week or two. She wished her friends hadn't died. She wished—hot breath invaded her space. And then, a nose nestled against her neck. She smiled, but she ignored Matzuka until his muzzle turned to nuzzle against her harder. She chuckled and reached up a hand to let the shepherd know he was getting the attention he craved. Or maybe he thought she needed the cuddle. As she glanced over at Carter, she caught him with his lips tilted up.

"Just because I like animals," she said, "doesn't mean I like your method of doing things."

"Maybe not, but it gets things done."

"True, but it reminds me a little too much of the Long-fellows. They just reach out and take whatever they want."

"The same thing *maybe* but for entirely different reasons," he said. "I came here on a mission to make sure the dog was being taken care of. Being beaten wasn't *being cared for*."

"But you didn't know that before you took the dog," she protested.

"I didn't need to," he said. "The spiked collar and the way Harold yanked on the leash were enough red flags. That dog was being used for intimidation tactics. If Harold ever learned the commands to make the dog kill, then we would have had a whole new issue here. And this dog could have been put down because of Harold's misuse of those commands."

"Are there really commands for that?"

"You better believe it. Attack commands. We don't *want* these War Dogs to kill. But, if one of our own men were in trouble, the War Dogs' specific training to counter that attack wouldn't be aimed for a shoulder. It'd be for the throat."

"They really are man's best friend, aren't they?"

"They can be," he said with a nod. "Unless you're on the wrong side of that best friend."

"And in the hands of somebody like Harold …"

"Exactly. We really don't want to get into an argument with the local street thugs, but—"

"Too late," she said. "But then, by now, I think you've gotten into a war with several people around here already, haven't you?"

"No. Not at all. Not if you compare it to the true war coming up."

Just something about his voice had her looking at him in worry. "You won't get too badly involved, will you?"

"Nope, not too badly. I find it much better to nip this in the bud first."

"Nip what in the bud?"

"Intimidation, bullying," he said. "Because obviously way too much of that is going on. Somebody named Longfellow decides they want something, and they get it. That'll stop now."

In a gentle voice, she said, "I hate to be the one to tell you, but you're using the same tactics."

"Sure, but for different reasons, different purposes. I know right from wrong," he said cheerfully, "and I know what's mine and what's not mine."

CARTER CHUCKLED TO himself, knowing Hailey didn't understand his military training was more of an offensive bent than a defensive maneuver. He had been trained to stop the opposition, not to let them continue on. He had learned a long time ago to seize life with both hands and to make it happen. Sitting around and waiting for it to happen would never sit well with Carter. That had been part of his problem with his recovery in the hospitals—waiting for his body to heal, something that was out of his control, outside of giving it as much rest, nutrition, and as little stress as possible. He'd been impatient, wanting his body to fix itself and fast.

His thoughts returned to the present situation. Since he'd arrived, he'd realized the town had gone to shit over the last two years, and some serious repercussions need to happen in response to all that. One of those was the fact that his buddy's ranch was in serious trouble with these Longfellows cutting fences to poach cattle and probably to squat on Gordon's property. The Longfellow family had been here in this area for probably over a century, who all seemed to be genetically born with the idea that everyone else here were their serfs and that the Longfellows could do what they wanted.

Carter wasn't too worried about the minor street thug, Harold, who was also a Longfellow. If need be, Carter would have a little talk with him. Now the more pressing matters were the land-encroaching issue and, of course, the murders of Hailey's two partners, which Carter highly suspected were all about bringing her down. Not necessarily bringing her down in terms of killing her but by destroying her business with the deaths of her partners, thereby losing clients, maybe even leading to lawsuits against her company, forcing her to pay out any judgments rendered against the company.

Maybe even to the extent that she would put up her family's ranch for sale.

"You and your brother still own the ranch equally?"

"Yes. Why?"

"Because," he said, "a result that could come out of this

murder-suicide is clients lacking confidence in the company. You could end up with lawsuits and the loss of your business. Potentially, you might be in a position where you have to sell your half of the ranch too to pay off any judgments rendered."

"That's not happening," she said quickly. "Our business was set up to protect each of the partners from personal loss. And my partnership equity was cash from my savings account, not my ranch as collateral. So my homestead is not tied to my business in any form or fashion. Even if I lost the company due to the deaths of my partners—even if I lost my reputation as a financial guru over this somehow—I could just retire. I would be fine living off the interest on my investments."

"The ranch is paid for?"

She nodded. "Has been for decades."

"I'm trying to figure out what motive the Longfellows might have for involving you in this."

"Maybe I'm the fall guy for the murders, ending up in jail, thinking they'll run the business in my absence. Failing that, maybe I'm the third partner to die, and the employees or whoever scramble to take over the place, not knowing I've tied up the succession of the business should I be killed too. Or you could consider it doesn't involve me, but I'm just collateral damage."

"It doesn't feel like that. Not when you're the last remaining partner in your finance company *and* also part owner of a ranch where the Longfellows are trying to take over your land."

"True, but wouldn't that then mean this takeover event should be also directed at Gordon?"

"Yes." Carter motioned up ahead, remembering the earlier incident on the road. They were near the ranch. "What do you think those vehicles were doing, surrounding you in a pincer move?"

"Punks playing games."

"You are—or were, as the case may be—their boss," he said drily.

"Yeah, but I don't have any proof, just my word that it was them."

"I took pictures of their license plates," he said. "So, let's share this with Raleigh and see if your sheriff is really bound by his oath or if he is more swayed by money and influence."

As Carter turned off the engine in the driveway, Hailey's phone rang. It was the sheriff. "Sheriff, what's up?"

"You just keep getting yourself into trouble, don't you?" His voice was testy.

"What is it now?"

"Believe it or not, somebody said your buddy there kidnapped a dog off the street."

"Carter's here," she said, putting her phone on Speaker.

"Harold had the K9 from the war department, confirmed by its own tattoo," Carter said. "And it's obviously been abused."

"That does help your case." Raleigh sighed. "I've also had complaints about Harold intimidating people with a dog and getting the dog to attack to make people pay up."

"Exactly," Carter said. "You should be thanking me for removing one problem in your life."

"I'm not ready to thank you yet," the sheriff said. "That guy's dangerous. You watch yourself."

"No problem. Let him come." Carter paused before continuing, "You should know that I fought in several wars in the Middle East. Over there, we knew who the enemy was.

But here? Here, it seems to come from the founding family, the Longfellows. I think your town sucks from that aspect, Sheriff."

"I'm starting to think the same thing," Raleigh answered in a tired voice. "I've managed to walk the fine line and keep the peace for a lot of years, but I knew this time would come."

"The time where you get to choose a side," Carter said with a half laugh, though he was deadly serious.

"No need to choose a side," Raleigh said. "I took an oath, and I have never broken it. But the Longfellows are making my life more complicated now."

Carter said, "Yeah, like Andy and Slim playing road games with Hailey earlier today." Carter went on to explain and also sent the sheriff the photos of the license plates of the two vehicles involved. "Like all the attacks on Gordon's cattle and land?"

"Yes," the sheriff said with a huge sigh. "Make sure you keep him safe, will you?"

"Meaning?" Hailey asked.

"Meaning, I overheard a conversation today saying that you were already taken care of, Hailey. They were outside my office but by the time I got there to see who was speaking they were gone. Now they just had to make sure Gordon wasn't any trouble. That's the reason for my call. I've been ringing Gordon's cell for the last ten minutes, but I'm not getting any answer."

Both Carter and Hailey jumped from the truck and rushed into the house.

"Shit," Carter said. "You better hope they haven't already done something to Gordon because you know there will not be peace in this town for a long time to come." He passed the phone back to Hailey with the sheriff still on the other end. Then pulled out his own. "Geir, get me backup ASAP at Gordon's ranch."

"I've got a neighboring county's sheriff heading your way. Well, he was sent to speak to your sheriff, but I'll have him detour to the ranch."

"Just make it happen and fast. Gordon's MIA." And he ended the call and pocketed his phone.

"We're looking for Gordon now," Hailey told the sheriff.

"Let me know what you find, but I'm heading that way now." At that, Raleigh hung up.

Carter and Hailey continued their search through the house and out to the barns.

Carter called at the top of his lungs, "Gordon! Where are you?"

"The old Ford truck's missing," Hailey called out behind Carter. "That's the one Gordon drives most of the time to check the fence line. We need to take the horses."

"Or the truck I've been driving," he said, racing back to ranch truck parked to the side. He called Matzuka to his side. The dog eagerly jumped up into the box, eager to go with them.

She hopped in beside him. "But he may have gone off too far."

"This truck is no sissy. If your old Ford can get somewhere on this ranch, then so can this one." He turned on the engine and backed up.

"But that one's already beat to crap," she said in a dry tone.

"Absolutely no contest when it comes to choosing between losing this truck versus Gordon. Any idea where he went?"

"Probably to the disputed land."

"Is there any real dispute?"

"No," she said. "The markers are very clear."

"Give me directions." Carter headed the truck where she told him to go. "Any idea how much land the Longfellows have?"

"In town, they have a ton of it. But out here, they have less than we do."

"Any chance that's at the bottom of this? They might think they should have more than you because they are, after all, *Longfellows*?"

"Who the hell knows?" Hailey asked.

After that, they drove in silence for another five minutes.

"There's the old Ford!" Hailey pointed.

Carter raced toward it and pulled up behind it. However, they saw no sign of Gordon. Carter hopped out and checked the truck. "Nothing's here."

He looked around at the vast amount of mostly empty land with some brush and a copse of trees and a cut fence about forty to fifty feet away but no sign of anyone.

No sign of Gordon.

CHAPTER 9

"**A**ND THIS IS why we needed the horses," Hailey said, hands on her waist. "Now we have to go on foot." Hailey turned her gaze to the sky, and, sure enough, two birds circled.

"We don't have time to waste. Let's go," Carter said, pointing the dog to the old truck, to get a whiff of Gordon's scent.

With Matzuka at his side, she watched while Carter gave the dog instructions to find Gordon. It took Matzuka a few confused moments to figure out what he was asking, but, soon enough, he picked up on something and took off. Toward the birds circling above.

Hailey understood. With a cry, she followed Matzuka, keeping him in her sights. Carter raced at her side. She could see the impact of the prosthetic on his gait, but he never said a word. If anything, he moved faster.

"They better not have hurt him," she cried out, terrified of what she'd find ahead.

"Unfortunately three people are dead already," Carter said. "I don't think a fourth will matter much to them."

"Do you really think it's all related?" she asked, jogging beside him.

"I don't see how it can't be when this town is such a cesspool. Generally the shit all has to go down the same sewer."

"You have a colorful turn of phrase. And I really don't like it."

"Maybe not, but it doesn't change the fact that it might be the truth." He looked around at the ground. "These rocks aren't too big. We could have driven."

"We may have to," she said, "depending on how injured Gordon is."

They came up over a slight rise to see a body lying ahead of them. Matzuka reached the body, barked twice, and sat down beside it.

Hailey gasped and ran flat-out, arriving at her brother's side before Carter. He dropped down to her side, but she was already checking for a pulse.

"He's alive, but he's been shot." She stepped back to let Carter closer, her hand instinctively going to Matzuka, praising him for his work.

Carter checked his friend over. "I see one bullet wound in his hip, and he's been grazed by a bullet on the side of his head. That's the one that likely took him down, but the one at his hip is keeping him down."

Blood continued to sluggishly pump from Gordon's body. While Hailey checked Gordon's head wound, Carter ripped off his overshirt, popping every button loose, then took off his T-shirt and used it as a bandage. He tucked the cotton shirt into Gordon's jeans, right under the waistband, hoping to stop the bleeding. Realizing what he was doing, Hailey tugged her T-shirt over her head, leaving on her camisole, then folded the cotton shirt and placed the square of material into Gordon's pocket, right where the bullet wound gushed blood. Hopefully those two makeshift bandages would remain in place just by the support of

Gordon's jeans.

Her brother was in desperate need of medical attention. She glanced back at the truck. "Should have driven."

"No time to waste now," he said, slipping on his over-shirt that no longer buttoned up but could be used for further bandages as needed. He bent his prosthetic leg, knowing he shouldn't lift Gordon by himself. *To hell with that nonsense*, he thought.

Hailey watched, worry clearly in her mind as it showed up in her facial expression. She doubted his body was ready for Gordon's weight, but Carter slowly straightened up, Gordon in his arms. Her brother was no lightweight. He was easily two-hundred-plus pounds. And all muscle. It went with the ranching lifestyle.

Beside her, Carter called to the dog. "Matzuka, let's go. Back to the truck."

"I'll drive it closer," Hailey said as she raced ahead, the dog at her heels.

Carter didn't say a word. Then he probably couldn't. He kept his gaze locked on the uneven ground in front of him as he carried her brother toward the truck. She hopped inside and turned on the engine, wishing she could get closer faster and save him the extra steps. She could see the strain in his facial expression and in the wrinkles around his pinched lips.

"Open the tailgate," he called out. "I'll sit in the back with him. Matzuka up." Without more urging, the dog jumped up to the back and paced, whining as he approached carrying Gordon.

"That's hardly safe."

"No way to get him and me and the dog inside the truck. This isn't a four-door."

She followed his instructions and dropped the tailgate.

As she got back inside the cab, she caught sight of an old plaid shirt behind the seat. She slung that on, knowing she'd be driving straight into town, and she was just in her camisole and jeans. It covered her slightly but was in rough shape, covered in dried stains.

So, that was what they did. Awkwardly Carter sat against the side of the bed, the tailgate closed and shifted backward, trying not to bump his buddy but held him gently. Hailey opened the window between the cab and the bed as soon as she got in, then drove as fast as she could.

"Don't worry about us. I'll keep Gordon from bouncing around the best I can. Drive like hell straight to the hospital," Carter said.

"I am. I'm also calling it in."

CARTER LISTENED AS Hailey called the hospital first, letting them know Gordon was coming in with a bullet wound to his hip and a head injury. Her tone was calm, cool. Just like she'd been when they'd found Gordon. That she'd stripped off her shirt without a thought to help her brother said a lot. Her honey-glazed skin had glowed in the afternoon sun. It had been impossible to ignore the beautiful body before him, her breasts lovingly cupped in a soft white lace-tipped camisole. At the same time, it was her direct no-nonsense approach that had impressed him much more.

Meanwhile, Carter called Geir to update him.

"Puts Hailey in the crosshairs next. I've got two more uniforms coming your way."

Carter didn't bother getting details. "Send one to the hospital. The other to the ranch to relieve the nearby county sheriff." He was just happy to have armed backup who weren't related to the Longfellows. Then Carter heard Hailey on the phone again. Talking to the sheriff this time.

"Heads up, Sheriff," she said, her voice hard and gritty. "The war's just hit town. They shot Gordon."

Even in the back of the cab, Carter heard Raleigh swear. However, the last thing the sheriff told Hailey was to not do anything stupid.

Hailey laughed at that. "Doing *nothing* is stupid. Defending ourselves is not stupid. We've got a lot of dead people and one more they intended to leave for dead. They'll pay for each and every one."

Then she shut off the phone, leaving both Carter and probably the sheriff to wonder at her tone.

But then again, she was dealing with, first, the loss of her business partners and now her remaining family member being attacked.

"Geir has three law enforcement types headed our way. One is a sheriff in a nearby county, to talk some sense into Raleigh."

"Won't be soon enough," Hailey grumbled, followed by a growl.

"I had him redirect one to the hospital and one to the disputed land area, leaving the out-of-town sheriff to deal with Raleigh."

She nodded, yet focused on driving faster and faster.

Carter would help out at the ranch to maintain things while Gordon was out. Temporarily out. Just temporarily. Carter wouldn't even contemplate the possibility of him dying. Gordon was too vibrant a man. He grabbed his phone from his pocket and redialed Geir. As soon as he answered, Carter added, "I have the dog too."

The dog was in the bed with him, lying right beside Gordon. Its head was on his shoulder.

"Wow," Geir said. "Shit really hit the fan, didn't it?"

"Yeah. I'm not armed, but I'll be supplying myself from Gordon's rifle collection at the ranch."

"Do what you gotta do."

As soon as Geir hung up, Carter phoned Debbie. "Debbie, Gordon's been shot."

She screamed at the other end of the phone, not even finding the words to say anything.

"Meet us at the hospital," he said. "One bullet hit his hip, and he has a head wound. I don't know if he has other injuries. I hope not because we're in the back of a pickup right now."

Then, as if a plug suddenly stopped her emotions, she spoke calmly and businesslike. "What's your ETA?"

"About ten minutes. We've put them on alert, but—"

"I'll meet you there," she said before she hung up.

Carter sank and looked at his friend's waxy pale skin. "Damn it, Gordon, you better make it through this."

No answer came from his buddy. Not even a whimper or a jolt in his facial expression. Gordon was out cold, his body struggling to survive. Carter wondered how long Gordon had been lying there on his land, unnoticed. The sooner his injuries got medical care, the better. Once the body started shutting down, nobody could do much of anything.

Carter closed his eyes, waiting for the trip to end. But it was interminable. He'd been on the receiving end himself, in a similar truck ride, when his team had hauled his ass back to the camp medic during that nightmare mission in Iraq. Half conscious, half unconscious, wishing he were dead. It was torture every time they lost their balance, swayed, and knocked his injured body.

Finally Hailey pulled up into the emergency area, and a medical team ran toward them. They opened the tailgate, and Carter handed off Gordon onto the gurney as gently as he could. Within seconds, the team raced away with Gordon, and Hailey glanced at Carter.

"I'd go in, but I'm barely presentable or germ-free," she said with a half smile. "We need to go home and grab some stuff for both of us and clothes for Gordon. Then we can return with my wheels to stay with Gordon."

Carter looked at his blood-stained clothing, then nodded.

Two marked vehicles pulled up, sirens blaring and lights flashing, and the drivers of each approached them, identifying themselves. Carter sent one inside the hospital and asked the other one to follow them to the ranch. With a nod, he got back into his vehicle.

"And I've got to feed Matzuka here," he said to Hailey. He reached out to pet the shepherd who now whimpered at his side, lying down half on the tailgate and half on the truck bed. "This has been rough on him too."

"I'd say so," Hailey said in a dry tone. "Let's get you two into the cab and get home. Then we can split up and do what we need to do."

Carter hopped down, bringing the dog with him. "I'll drive back. We should pick up the old ranch truck too."

She hesitated. "If it's even running."

"It's possible they disabled it, but instead they disabled him, so I don't think they gave a shit about the vehicle."

"Good. We're obviously heading into trouble and an extra pair of wheels is never a bad option."

It took them twenty minutes to head back, another half hour to show the officer the disputed area, leaving him there to guard the fence, while Carter drove the old Ford back to the house and Hailey drove the other truck. After another twenty minutes, both had showers and had changed into clean clothes.

Once done, Hailey had a small bag packed with a change of clothes for Gordon and her laptop. She looked at Carter and said, "I don't know what's happening at the office right now, but my brother is obviously my priority." She stepped out of the front door and headed down the driveway.

Carter followed her. "I haven't got the bug-detection stuff yet," he said. "I'll take care of sweeping your offices when it arrives."

She hesitated, then pulled out her spare keys. "This is Gordon's set. If you need it to get inside the office, use it." And then she hopped into her truck.

Carter shook his head and said, "I wish you'd wait half an hour. I don't want to send you in alone."

"I'm just going to the hospital."

"Be careful. I need to feed the dog. Don't suppose you have a leash here?"

She laughed. "Nope. Herd dogs don't work on leashes."

"I'll get some rope for Matzuka from the barn. I probably don't need that, but being prepared is better. Then, after that, I'll head back into town myself."

"You can always talk to me on the phone," she said. "I don't think anybody else will attack me at this stage."

"But you don't know that."

She shook her head. "No, I don't." She forcibly closed the driver's side door, pushing him out of the way. "I'll let you know when I get there."

Hailey backed out and took off, leaving Carter to watch her for a few more moments before getting on with his business.

Hating that she was taking off on her own, Carter went inside the house to the back, exiting onto the rear porch. There he grabbed a water bowl and a dog food bowl and, as an added bonus, found a short piece of rope discarded in a corner, which saved him a trip to the barn. He went to the guest bedroom to retrieve the dog food he had brought with him and some bottled water. That covered what Matzuka needed.

Next he gathered his laptop, phone, and wallet. He passed by the rifle cabinet in the front room, nodding. Five rifles and plenty of ammo. Good. With all this shit going on, he needed to make sure he set that damn laptop up and to run his program. There were too many things going wrong and they need to know who was behind it all. He could make a quick detour. The company was still closed. He could whip in and set it up then race to the hospital.

He opened the front door and whistled for the dog. Matzuka came flying outside. Carter climbed into the truck, and Matzuka jumped up into the cab, sitting by his side, more than happy to go for a truck ride.

Carter laughed. "Obviously you're a traveling type of guy."

He gave a light bark, and Carter laughed some more. With all the crap going on, no way he wanted to leave this innocent ball of brightness alone. While driving, he called Geir and caught him up on the mess.

"Did you manage to get the shipment yet?" Geir asked.

"I'll grab it now. There hasn't been time to do anything but put out fires so far. This town is going to hell way too damn fast."

"I'm still trying to locate even more backup." Geir's tone was sharp.

Carter hesitated, then said, "Could use all the help you can muster up. The local sheriff and his deputies are all Longfellow-related. They just shot Gordon and left him for dead. I'm not armed in the conventional way, but I've got Matzuka with me for now. Later I'll arm up, thanks to Gordon's gun cabinet at home."

"Maybe those Longfellows have crossed a line, and you could create a civilian army with the townsfolk."

"That's possible too. Meantime, I just wish I knew where the sheriff stood."

"He's a typical elected official. Only one place he can sit comfortably. That's on the fence, trying to keep from getting his ass kicked off the job."

"Then he'd better have decent balance because I'll knock him off his perch if he doesn't lean in the right direction."

CHAPTER 10

H AILEY WAS HALFWAY to the hospital when she noticed a truck pulling up behind her. Sure enough, it was Carter. He must have really busted his ass to catch up to her. But still, the sense of relief she felt was hard to ignore. Not only had their relationship turned a corner but so had everything in her life. It wasn't a corner she liked though. She parked at the hospital and walked inside.

"How's Gordon?" she asked the receptionist.

The woman looked up at her and frowned. "The hip wound's bad. I think they're prepping him for surgery. Go on through to emergency and talk to somebody there."

Hailey headed inside, then stopped when she realized Carter was looking at her. She motioned for him to come too, but the receptionist called out, "Family only."

"Yep, I know." She reached out a hand, and Carter grasped it. They stepped into the emergency room and waited until they found somebody. "Where's Gordon?"

The doctor motioned to the far corner. "We're taking him up to surgery in about an hour. We've got him stabilized, and he's holding."

"The head injury?"

"It doesn't look that bad. We've done X-rays. We're more worried about the hip."

"With good reason," Carter said. "Can we see him?"

The doctor nodded and brought them to the appropriate cubicle, where a uniformed officer stood on duty. Thankfully not one of the local Longfellow deputies. The doc nodded to the officer and then pulled back the curtain. "You can spend a few minutes with him, but we'll send him up to pre-op soon."

Hailey rushed to her brother's side and slipped her fingers through his. She reached down and kissed his cold forehead and whispered against his hair, "Dammit, Gordon. You pull out of this, you hear me?"

But there was no answer. No flinching, no nothing. She studied her brother's lax skin. Her brother had always seemed so solid and so stable, one of those men who would be around forever. She never imagined him like this. She felt the tears collect in the corner of her eyes. She brushed them away, fingers rubbing hard against her skin. She hadn't even had a chance to say goodbye.

"He's going to surgery now," an orderly said, as they moved his bed toward the hallway. The cop joined them.

Carter snagged her up and tucked her out of the way, keeping his arms around her.

She didn't mind right now. In fact, she felt herself sinking deeper into his embrace. Something was so devastating about watching her only living relative, a brother she adored, being wheeled away for surgery. She looked up at Carter. "I'll stay."

"Maybe you could stay upstairs," he told her. "There should be a waiting room close to surgery."

She turned to a doctor nearby, who was talking to another nurse. "Is that possible?"

"There are several waiting rooms. If you ask the receptionist or one of the nurses, we could notify you when he's out."

"Good enough," she said. She walked to the emergency desk and left her name and number, then asked about where she could wait.

"Sounds like you probably need a cup of coffee," the woman said sympathetically. "You can go to the cafeteria and then up to the second floor and sit in one of the waiting areas there."

Hailey, under the curious eyes of the receptionist, barely noticed how much interest she was garnering. Likely because of Carter's presence. "I don't know what you need to do," she told Carter, "but, if you want to stay, you can too."

"It's already late, and I have to make a few phone calls and check up on a few things. Plus I left Matzuka in the truck to eat and drink something. I'll come back in about an hour?" She nodded, and he led her to the cafeteria. "Are you okay to eat here?"

"I need food because I need energy," she muttered. "I need energy in order to make it through this ordeal. But I really don't care what I eat."

"I understand that, but if nothing here appeals, I can always bring something in."

"I'll have a muffin and some coffee for now. If you feel like picking something up, just bring it to the second floor waiting room."

"Will do." He leaned over and dropped a kiss on her forehead, a complete and out-of-the-blue moment, and disappeared.

Hailey stood, stunned, her mind consumed with that kiss. Talk about having turned a corner but for all the wrong reasons. She paid for her coffee and muffin and then tried to find a place to wait for her brother. A waiting room was just outside the OR, and several other families there were barely holding it together. She found herself a spot in the corner and sat down. However, as soon as she had a chance to sit, she recognized one of the women barely holding herself together on the far side. "Debbie?"

Debbie took one look at her and raced to her side, throwing her arms around her. "I didn't see you come in," she whispered.

Hailey shook her head and hugged her sister-in-law. "I think we're both in a daze."

"Is there anywhere we can talk in private?" Debbie asked.

"A couple benches are in the hallway, if you want."

The two women moved to the hallway where they wouldn't disturb the other families.

"Tell me what happened," Debbie demanded.

Hailey shrugged. "I don't know what to tell you." She did her best to fill Debbie in. When she finally fell silent, Debbie just stared at her with wide eyes.

"Holy crap," she said. "Carter contacted me, so I knew he was in town. But I didn't know about the dog. He just went up to that damn drug dealer and stole him?"

"Yes," Hailey said, her lips twitching. "As if he knew exactly what he was doing."

"I think, in a way, he did, didn't he?"

"I knew he was navy, but since when did a seaman have anything to do with that kind of stuff?"

Debbie lowered her voice. "He told me that he was in a special elite team in the navy."

At that, Hailey settled back. "That makes sense, but how come I didn't know?"

"Because you avoided him at every turn," Debbie said,

giving her a crooked grin.

"So true, but apparently we're on different terms now."

"Good. It's about time. You've loved that man since forever."

Hailey winced. "Is it that obvious?"

"Only to me, probably," Debbie said. "Nobody's that prickly around somebody unless they're deliberately trying to distance themselves."

"He broke my heart when he got married," Hailey admitted. "I'd already been pretty prickly to him before that because he obviously didn't give a shit about me prior to that time, but when he got married ..." She shook her head and popped a chunk of muffin into her mouth. That way, she didn't have to talk.

"I was worried about you back then," Debbie said. Then she stopped and looked at her. "Where's Carter's wife now?"

"Gone," Hailey said. "I'm not sure I understand the circumstances. She just walked out on him about two years ago, never to return."

"Probably when she realized he was injured. She was that kind of woman. Since when did *'til death do us part* become *until I don't like the shape you're in?*"

"It doesn't matter now," Hailey said. "Gordon's the only one who matters."

Debbie nodded. "I can't believe this happened."

"The Longfellows have been pushing the land issue aggressively this year. And I don't know, but Gordon might have been more aggressive in his response this time too."

"Not Gordon," Debbie said. "That's not him."

"No, it's not him *usually*," Hailey said. "But, since you left, he's been angrier and more morose. Despondent, even."

Debbie winced. "And yet he's never asked me to come

back. So maybe he doesn't really give a shit."

"Oh, I know he does," Hailey said. "And I know Carter's been talking to him since he arrived too. Gordon just doesn't know what to do about it. He wants a family, but he doesn't agree with getting tested or with IVF. Probably the whole male ego problem in potentially knowing the fault is his."

Debbie grimaced and nodded.

"As for adoption or a surrogate, I don't know how he feels about that."

"I want a family," Debbie said, "but I never said it had to be ours. I know other methods are available, but we'd have to start with testing, both of us, including him getting his sperm tested to see if it's viable or not."

"I don't know how you initially asked him about it, but that may have set him up to feeling less like a man. And, for Gordon, that's one of the few things he's fairly vehement about."

Debbie chuckled. "Isn't that the truth?" Then she sobered up quick. "How sad that we're in this situation."

"I know," Hailey said. "The company is a mess too after Fred's and Phil's deaths."

"Oh my, yes. I can't believe both Fred and Phil are dead. They were icons in this town."

"Right. It's been a shitty day. I don't know what the latest theory is, but it's possible Phil killed both Betty and Fred and then turned the gun on himself."

"But why would he do that?"

"I don't know," Hailey said. "I was hoping the sheriff would check into Phil's medical records."

"Of course," Debbie said, raising her pointer finger. "He had pancreatic cancer. I talked to Betty about it a month ago. The cancer had advanced, so he was looking at about nine months to live. But why would he rush it?"

Hailey stared in shock. "I didn't know about that. Why didn't he say anything?"

"Probably hadn't come to terms with it himself," Debbie said. "Betty said he was really struggling."

"Of course he'd be struggling! But we needed to put things into place for the company."

"I think he felt the company would be fine without him, and he was the one who could afford to disappear."

"But then why kill Fred?"

"That one, I don't get," Debbie said. "And nobody'll convince me that's what Phil did either. Yet, I hate to say it, but I *can* see him shooting Betty and taking his own life. And I can also see Betty agreeing to it."

Hailey was stunned. "But why?"

Debbie continued, "I don't know what Betty's health was like, but they've been together for over fifty years. I know Betty said she had no life without him. So, they might have made a pact."

Hailey slumped in place. "I never thought of that," she whispered. "How sad."

"But it's also ..." Debbie hesitated. "I know this might sound wrong, but, I mean, it's also a show of love, isn't it? You don't want to be left behind. I think that's got to be the worst thing."

"Yet you left Gordon behind," Hailey said bluntly. She couldn't stop the words coming out of her mouth. It sounded accusing, and, the worst thing was, she understood why Debbie did it, yet she still said it. She'd always side with her brother, she realized.

"That was a low blow," Debbie whispered, her expression devastated.

"They're all low blows here lately," Hailey said sadly. "Every single one of these is a very low blow. How are we supposed to deal with any of it?"

"I have no clue. We really need the sheriff to step up and give us an idea of what's going on."

"But why would he?" Hailey asked. "He's still trying to investigate. He has no answers yet."

"I haven't come up with any motivation for Phil to kill Fred. I just can't see him doing it." Debbie asked after a while. "That doesn't make any sense."

"I know. I've been wondering about that one myself."

"Could there be any chance Fred knew about Phil's cancer and what Phil was going to do, and so Fred decided that taking his own life was a good idea too?"

Hailey stared at her, shaking her head. "Why would he do that though?"

"I don't have a clue why anybody would commit suicide because I've never been in a situation like that, but I guess suicides do happen in clumps, don't they? A lot of people bring that thought up in their mind after somebody they know, particularly a celebrity, does it. So, given the fact that Phil may have told Fred what Phil and his wife would do, to prepare Fred for what the company would suffer through, then Fred did the same thing?"

"And then *neither* of them discussed this with me to prepare for handling the business thereafter?" Hailey shook her head, her lips pursed. "I just don't see it. Okay, the murder-suicide between Phil and Betty, as some Romeo and Juliet pact, I *guess* I could imagine. But Fred? ... I would have thought he'd gone out with, you know, a blaze."

Debbie tilted her head. "In a way, he did go out in a

blaze. Particularly as it looks like he was murdered. I'm hearing rumors about that, not just from you here and now, but I don't know for certain."

"I know," Hailey said. "But, unless Fred had some medical condition, I can't see him taking the easy way out by committing suicide."

"I don't think there's anything easy about suicide," Debbie said calmly. "I've known two people who took that route. One of them did it because she had a terminal illness and couldn't deal with it. She didn't want her family to suffer along with her. She ended up overdosing on drugs and shortening the process."

"I'm sorry," Hailey said. "I'm not myself, and I've never been in that situation, so it's hard for me to contemplate. I didn't mean to judge these people, but I sure wouldn't want to be left behind. I'd want all the time I could have with them. I just … I just don't know anything anymore."

Debbie nodded and continued, "Also Fred and Phil would have known the company was in good hands. Look at you. You're the star of the place."

"I'm certainly the junior partner, with all their years of experience, but I don't know about being a star."

"You are, whether you want to be or not. Both men knew it. You were the New Age analyst. You were the digital version of them. You were the younger generation. Plus, neither of them had families anymore."

"Phil had Betty. Fred had an extended family," Hailey said with a sigh. "That's hardly fair."

"But not a family he particularly cared about leaving his company to," Debbie said gently. "That's why, when you were brought in, they made the decision to have the company go to you. I know Phil was good with that choice. I spoke to Betty many times. She thought you were the best thing for Phil because he was finally looking at retiring, knowing he could because the company he spent so many years at would be okay."

Hailey couldn't stop the warm glow swelling in her heart. "That's really nice to know. Too bad they didn't tell me that when they were still alive."

Debbie laughed. "I don't think people ever do. They give compliments in roundabout ways instead of saying it outright and explaining how they feel."

"So true," Hailey said, "and I guess we're the same. I never told Carter how I felt. I just sat on the sidelines and watched while he married somebody totally wrong for him. I didn't know how he would have taken my interference back then."

"Maybe you could have changed the course of his life."

"I doubt it," Hailey said. And then she smiled. "I wouldn't have the company if I had."

"Another good point. Are you keeping all the staff?"

Hailey shook her head "I haven't a clue. But, with the undercurrents at work, I do need to make some staffing changes. Two of the guys are trouble. That's Slim and Andy, but I've already had to fire Slim."

She explained what they had done on the road, and Debbie stared at her in horror. "But you're their boss!"

"Exactly. I was also a female and driving alone on a country road. Whether they knew it was me doesn't matter. It was a real shit move. That's not the people I want working for me," Hailey said. And then she sighed and buried her face in her hands. "But I also know people are looking at me sideways because of my partners' deaths. Some are speculating I killed them."

"Hopefully a suicide note or something was left to help clarify things."

Hailey didn't mention the fact the gun was in the wrong hand for Fred to have committed suicide. In Phil's and his wife's cases, Hailey hoped it was a clear-cut case of murder-suicide so no further doubts remained as to what happened to the couple. She kept her face buried.

"You know something? I've always wondered about that," Debbie said. "If I would do something like that, I would leave a clear explanation of why I committed suicide. And also what I was thinking before doing it."

"I think that would be true for most people," Hailey said. "I'm not sure about Phil. Or Fred. Both were very private, now that I think about it."

Debbie frowned. "Betty, on the other hand, no way she wouldn't have told the world."

"Would she have put something like a delayed time for a post on Facebook or an email to be sent?" Hailey asked.

"I doubt it, but I could look into it."

"If you could, that would help a lot," Hailey said as she slumped in her seat. "I'm sitting here wondering if Gordon's shooting is related to the deaths in the company."

"Oh my," Debbie said. "I didn't even consider that because I thought they were initially deemed as suicides."

"Exactly," Hailey said with a wry twitch of her lips. "So, if we knew for sure one was a suicide, we wouldn't have to connect it to the other cases."

"Let me call someone who's a close friend of hers. See if she saw anything on social media," Debbie said. "I'll move down the hall. You'll let me know if there's any news on Gordon?"

Hailey nodded. "Don't worry. I'll get you immediately."

And she watched Debbie walk away. When she came back, she shook her head. "There was no suicide post."

CARTER WAS IN town, collecting his parcel at the post office, updating Geir and getting updates from Geir, stopping for food for him and Hailey. If she didn't want it, Matzuka seemed interested in the smells coming from the to-go bag. It was now fairly late, and he hoped Gordon had gone in for surgery. He imagined Hailey sitting there, fussing.

He touched base with her while Carter put Matzuka through his paces as they walked. Carter had the rope but hadn't put it on him yet. There didn't seem to be a need. He hadn't seen any signs of aggression, and the dog followed his hand commands beautifully. He wished he knew a little more of his history.

"Thanks, but I can't eat," Hailey said, then ended their call, not knowing anything yet on Gordon.

Carter sent Geir a text so he could figure out what Matzuka liked and didn't like, to make his transition easier. He obviously liked hamburgers, as he gobbled up Hailey's portion.

Carter had absolutely no intention of giving up this dog. Particularly because he was the one who had pinpointed Gordon out in the field. Other dogs were at the ranch, but they were herding dogs. Matzuka was well trained in other aspects. Carter just didn't know what specific aspects those were. Obviously, search-and-rescue was one of his skills. Carter knew a lot of the military K9s did that to help flush out insurgents in abandoned towns.

As he walked along, somebody called out, "Hey, what

kind of dog is that?"

He turned and smiled at the older woman, who frowned at Matzuka. "A retired War Dog," he said. "He gave five years of his life to sniff out bombs and to help our soldiers fight in Iraq."

The woman's face lit up in joy. "Really? I've never met one."

"Yeah, not too many of them managed to get back stateside. He's retired and looking forward to a few calm years."

"Oh my, yes." She stepped forward hesitantly. "May I say hi?"

"Sure," he told the old woman. Then he gave Matzuka the command to sit and told him that she was a friend. Matzuka sat. The woman reached out and nudged Matzuka with her fingers. The dog leaned in for more, looking for a bit of a rub.

The older lady, who had to be close to eighty, laughed. "He's beautiful." She spent a few more moments admiring Matzuka before looking up at Carter. "You're Gordon's friend, aren't you?"

"Yes," he said. "And you're Donna Mari, aren't you?"

She laughed in delight. "We have met a couple times but not for some years." She motioned to his hand. "Obviously the past few years were rough on you."

"Yeah, but now I'm back visiting with Gordon and Hailey."

"Lovely people," she said. "Absolutely lovely people. It's too bad about the Longfellows."

"Which ones?" he said in a dry tone.

She nodded. "Exactly. You've got to hit them at the heart to stop them because, when you cut one head off, another one grows."

"Oh," he said. "I remember. You're the notary in town, aren't you?"

"I used to be. I'm retired now," Donna Mari said. "But I heard from Debbie about how she and Gordon and Hailey were having some land disputes out there."

"Yes, and it's gotten much worse since Debbie left," Carter said. "I'm still trying to figure out how to handle it."

"The Longfellows are not all bad news, but the ones who are, are terrible. Whatever you do, make sure you take them out permanently."

"Like how they just tried with Gordon?" he asked softly.

Her sharp hawk eyes zeroed in on his. "They shot Gordon?"

"I found him out by the disputed lands with a bullet in his hip and a head wound."

She frowned. "My son and my nephew are law enforcement in the county one over if you ever need a hand."

"We need a hand," he blurted out. "The sheriff is between a hot spot and a hard place."

"He's a good man," the woman said, "but his deputies are a little too close to the Longfellows for my liking."

"Would your family help the sheriff?"

"Yes. He should call on them. He knows them himself."

"He might not know if he can count on his deputies," Carter said. "Maybe a gentle nudge would help him realize he has options."

She looked up and smiled. "I'll get right on that." She turned and walked away, but then remembered something. "Did you take that dog off the drug dealer, as rumor has it?"

"A possible drug dealer, yes, I did. Dogs like this can't be used for intimidation. They can be killers. Plus Matzuka deserves to retire, not to prey on the homeless or the kids who have gone down a rough path. Not to mention the fact Harold had beaten Matzuka with a belt or something."

"Start cleaning up the town now. And let me call our sheriff to remind him of the officers in my family."

Her phone call was short and to the point. She wasn't nearly as nice to the sheriff as she had been to Carter. He kind of felt sorry for the guy.

"Now you made a good start with the dog. That's a rescue which needed to happen."

"Glad you think so," he said, smiling at the determined woman.

"I'm glad to hear you're making this place your home."

He wasn't sure what she was talking about, but somehow he suspected the gossip mill had been working overtime.

As she started to walk away once again, she added one more thing. "Now, would you finally marry that Hailey girl and put her out of her misery?"

Then, she was gone, leaving him staring after her with an open mouth.

CHAPTER 11

HAILEY SAT BY Gordon's side at the hospital. He had come through the surgery and was now in recovery, but he hadn't woken up yet. She really needed him to wake up and to let her know he was okay. Just the thought of losing him was too much right now. Just then, Gordon shifted in the bed. She reached across gently and stroked his fingers. "Hey, Gordon. It's me. Take it easy."

One of the nurses walked in to check on him. She checked his vitals and smiled. "He starting to come out of it."

"Good," Hailey said. "It's been a pretty rough ride."

"Yes, but he's doing fine."

Hailey looked up to see Debbie walk in just then.

"How is he?" she asked the nurse abruptly.

"Just starting to regain consciousness," the nurse said.

Debbie sat down and gripped Gordon's other hand tightly. "Stupid idiot," she muttered.

"I don't think he asked for this," Hailey said.

"No, he didn't. But, at the same time, he did. Have you talked to the sheriff at all about that land problem?"

Hailey nodded. "And he's gone and talked to the Long-fellows about it, but they said they had nothing to do with it."

"So, they hired somebody to do it. Or they just plain

lied," Debbie said. "You know that's what's going on."

"It's possible. I don't know. I've never had a problem with Donnie before."

"How long has he had that land next to yours?"

"I think close to seventeen years, which is why I don't know why, all of a sudden, he would start causing trouble. Except it might not be him. His son Manfred moved in, maybe with his boys too, but I don't know that for sure. It makes sense though, as Donnie has gotten on in years. He might be eighty-something now."

"Who knows?" Fatigue was in Debbie's voice. She glared at Gordon, but her voice cracked as she spoke. "You better wake up. You are not leaving me because of this."

Hailey could see her sister-in-law was at the breaking point. Hailey sank back in her chair and checked her phone for messages. She sent Carter one too, asking where he was. He quickly answered that he was at the sheriff's office, looking for answers and for backup. And, no, there wasn't anything more to learn yet.

Sighing, she dropped the phone on her lap. "Come on, Gordon. Wake up," she snapped.

At that, his eyes flew open. And he stared around, puzzled. He rolled his head toward her. "Sis?"

She nodded and motioned to the other side. He rolled his head to the other side. She heard the breath leave his lungs.

"Debbie?" he croaked. "What happened?"

"You were shot," Hailey said calmly. She watched as he gripped Debbie's fingers hard, but his gaze zoomed back to her. "What?"

"We couldn't reach you, and the sheriff was worried that maybe somebody was coming after you, so we drove to where we thought you might be. We found the old truck, and then Matzuka, the dog, found you."

"Matzuka? Dog? Shot?"

Obviously he wasn't comprehending any of this. Hailey smiled, leaned over, and kissed him on the cheek. "Now that you're awake, I'll go get some fresh air."

Gordon and Debbie needed time alone. Whether this would help to heal the rift between them, Hailey didn't know, but having a third party at their first contact in months wasn't a good idea. Hailey walked down the hall and looked out the window and stared at the craziness of the land. She had spent her life here, loving it. She really didn't understand why they had these sudden problems on the ranch. She phoned Raleigh. "How old is Donnie now?"

"Maybe in his early eighties."

"And who gets the ranch if he goes? Manfred?"

"No clue," he said in surprise. "Why?"

"Because that might help me understand why, after seventeen years of peace, we're having the problems we are."

Raleigh sucked in a breath, understanding her comment. "Good point. I'll look into that."

"You should, considering that's where Gordon was when he was shot." Then she hung up on him.

She sat in a nearby chair and propped her elbows on the windowsill and thought about everything going wrong. It seemed connected to the Longfellows, but in what way did that connect her land to her business? Plus the missing K9. The fact that the dog was found with Harold Longfellow, even as an outcast in that family, was a coincidence she wasn't ready to accept. But then, when she thought about the percentage of the population here related in some way to the Longfellows and who did business with everyone in one way or another, it really wasn't surprising to find a tie-in. She didn't know how long she sat leaning against the window and staring out into nothing, but, when a voice jarred her from her pensive thoughts, and an arm slipped around her shoulder, she jerked up and stepped away.

Carter raised his hands. "Whoa. I did call out."

She frowned up at him and reached to rub her temples. "Sorry," she said with a shake of her head. "I was trying to figure this all out."

"Well, you have an incredibly impressive brain. I'm so sorry I disturbed you."

"No, it's not that. I just feel like it's all connected."

"It is, in the sense that one name keeps coming up. *Longfellow*."

"Right," she said. "But were they related to Phil's and Fred's issues? Because that stumps me."

"And yet you seem to think they're all related?"

"I want to go back to the office," she said suddenly. "Have you checked on the program you set up to run in my office?"

He shook his head. "No, but we can go back now if you want. I want to say hi to Gordon first though."

"Oh," she said, no longer as worried about her brother, given the fact he was now awake. "Please, let's go in. Debbie's here too, by the way."

A beaming smile crossed his face. "That's the best news I've heard all day." He pushed open the door and stepped in without warning. Right behind him, Hailey saw the couple separate quickly from their kiss.

With a fat smile at her sister-in-law, she said, "Carter wanted to say hi."

"Yeah," Carter said. "And then we're heading back to

Hailey's office."

"What will you find there?" Gordon challenged. "You're such a bookworm."

"And you're such a roughneck," Carter said back.

Gordon chuckled. "So not me. You know it doesn't fit."

"Neither does bookworm fit me, but we are who we are." Carter reached over and squeezed his friend's hand. "That was too damn close."

"I know."

"Did you see anybody before it happened?" Carter asked in a rush. "Any warning? Did you argue with someone? Anything?"

Hailey realized she hadn't even asked her brother that simple question. He'd been in such a daze when he woke up that he didn't even realize he'd been shot. All she'd been concerned about by then was him healing things with Debbie.

She turned her gaze back to her brother now and nodded. "Any information would be helpful."

"Honestly I don't feel like I had any warning. Nobody was there. I didn't see anything. I was just walking along the fence where another section had been cut, wondering what I should do about it and getting downright pissed. I had my hat off, and I lifted it up and put it on my head. Then it's like a fire lit across my head. I reached up my hand, and another one came, at my hip. After that, I don't remember anything."

"That was the two shots we found," Carter said. "From what direction?"

Gordon stopped for a minute and closed his eyes. "Off in the ridge. Not too far away but in that copse of trees there. It could easily hide somebody."

"I stopped to see your doctor, asking if I could take a look at the bullets, but he didn't want to let me. I told him that I knew guns and that I was trying to figure out what kind of weapon was used. He said it was on its way to forensics for testing."

"But that didn't stop you, did it?" Gordon asked with a smirk.

Carter gave him a smile. "After the doctor left, I went to the nurse and pretended to be somebody I wasn't. I can tell you the bullet's from a 30-30 lever action rifle, so somebody was very fast loading and firing."

"Or," Hailey said, "there were two shooters."

"It sucks," Gordon said, "but that is possible."

"It is, indeed," Carter agreed. "I'm sorry I wasn't there."

Gordon shook his head. "No need. The last thing I wanted was you babysitting me. That would have just gotten both of us shot."

The two best friends grinned at that. Hailey noticed Gordon getting fatigued. She grabbed Carter's arm, pulling him back. "Time to leave."

"I want you to stay safe in here, do you hear me?" Carter told Gordon.

He nodded. "I hear you."

Carter spoke softly to the uniformed officer standing guard outside Carter's room. The officer nodded, and Carter clapped him on the shoulder.

As they walked out of the hospital a few minutes later, Carter asked Hailey, "Do you want to slip into your office and take a look, or do you want to go straight home?"

She frowned and took several deep breaths of cool fresh air. Hospitals always had an off smell. "We should probably go to the office. At least to check on your program. I have the files at home, but I don't know if I'll have the energy or the concentration to work on them."

"Okay, let's go to your office first. I can always sweep for bugs too. I picked up the package I was waiting for at the post office." With that, he called for Matzuka to jump into the front of the truck and waited until she started up her truck and passed him leaving the parking lot. He followed her to her office.

As she hopped out, she was happy to see everything was as it should be. It was a weeknight, and nobody should be here. She undid the security and let them both in, then reset it. "Do you think we should leave Matzuka in the truck?"

Carter looked at her and raised an eyebrow. "We're only going to be a few minutes."

She shrugged. "The last thing I want is to have somebody follow us inside and shoot us."

"Good point," he said with a smile. "So let's go fast so we can go back to him."

Upstairs, Hailey walked into her office. She was glad the locks were still set. She walked over to her desk. "Nothing's changed here," she said.

"Nothing here either," Carter said as he checked the laptop where his software program continued to run. "That's all good."

Then she heard a footstep outside her office door and froze. Carter put a finger to his lips, and she nodded. He slipped toward the door and tilted his head against it, his eyes closed, as if listening. Gently he opened up the door and stuck his head out. And there was a tall, slim man.

He motioned her over, and she called out, "Slim, what are you doing here?"

Slim took one look at them and bolted.

Carter swore and tore after him. She realized how hard that must have been on his leg. He had already put it to heavy use today. She locked up her office and went to check the other offices. Fred's was unlocked. And they had locked that door with the key *and* had set the numerical keypad. She went inside and looked, but it didn't look any different. She checked on Phil's office as well.

After that, she tore after the men. By the time she reached them, Slim was on the ground, with Carter holding Slim's hands behind his back.

"Now we can add breaking and entering to your list of crimes," Carter said.

"Worthless." Slim sneered.

"That was you in that pincer move," he said. "You and your buddy, Andy. You were the ones with access to the offices."

"I didn't get anything," Slim said in a raw voice. "You took everything away."

"What's still here has been keyed differently," Hailey said, "yet you still got into the offices and that pisses me off."

She stepped off to the side and called Raleigh. "Sheriff, we've got another problem."

WHEN THE SHERIFF arrived, he swore as he saw Slim on the ground. He hitched his pants up higher on his waist and said, "What the hell did you do this time, Slim?"

Carter let Slim stand, and he waited to see if the sheriff would do the right thing.

"My understanding is you've been fired, and you're not allowed access to the property," Raleigh said.

"So what? Until I get my final paycheck, I still have rights."

"No, you don't," the sheriff said. He glared at Hailey. "I thought you already had everything changed."

"I did," she said. "So the question really is, how did Slim get in?"

The sheriff swore up and down. He took out his handcuffs and locked Slim in them. Then he searched Slim, took all his keys away from him, then led him to the back of the cruiser.

He secured Slim in the back seat, then stood closer to Hailey to have a private conversation. "I won't be able to hold him," he told her. "You have a reluctant and angry employee getting back into the building, but he didn't do any damage, did he?"

Carter shrugged. "No clue, we didn't have a chance to check yet."

"He had keys to both Phil's and Fred's offices," Hailey said indignantly. "The ones you just took off him and pocketed. Maybe he shot Fred."

From inside the sheriff's car, Slim yelled out, "I did not! He was family."

"Yeah, but family that was old and holding onto money, right?"

Slim glared at her.

She nodded. "Young punks like you don't ever want to wait for the older generation to pass on in their own time. You just wanted to give him a little help, didn't you?" At that, she smiled at him and made sure it wasn't a nice smile.

Carter almost wanted to cheer her on, but there was a limit. If Hailey lost her temper and attacked Slim, that would cross several lines.

"I need to know that you'll investigate Slim as a potential murder suspect and for breaking and entering alongside corporate espionage, maybe even money laundering and embezzling," Carter told the sheriff.

The sheriff pushed his hat off his head. "Well, now ..."

"Either you do your job," Carter said calmly, "or I'll bring in people above you."

The sheriff got angry.

"You can get as angry as you want, but, from what I see, your town's got a huge problem. And it'll get cleaned up with or without your help. It'll get cleaned up now."

"I've never taken any bribes," the sheriff said. "I always do my job. This is an official sheriff's matter. You are not a deputy or the sheriff. You can mind your own business."

At that, Carter gave him a smile that should have had the man running. He liked the fact that the sheriff stepped forward and glared at him instead.

"I'm glad to see you've got some balls," Carter said, "because you'll need them. If you don't charge Slim and keep him under arrest until you get the rest of your murder investigations taken care of ..." He left the threat undefined.

"There's nothing to suggest it was anything other than a murder-suicide," Raleigh said. His voice was low and hard. "And don't threaten me, or I'll throw you in jail along with him."

Carter nodded. "You know what? That's not a bad idea. I wouldn't mind a few days of beating up that piece of junk."

"You can't put him in the same cell with me," Slim roared.

"Why not? After all, you and Andy pulled that pincer move on Hailey," Carter said. "That's attempted murder as far as I'm concerned." He turned to face Raleigh.

The sheriff swore and looked at Slim. "Damn it, Slim. Why did you have to go do that? You're in a heap of trouble now."

"Plus, not too long afterward, Gordon was shot twice. Maybe by the same two guys who tried to box in Hailey on her way home to the ranch? They were right there close by."

Slim sank back, a sullen look on his face. That was all the answer Carter needed.

"Does that answer your question?" Carter looked at the sheriff with smugness.

The sheriff snorted in disgust, focused on Slim and, ignoring Carter, said, "You always were a piece of shit. I've been telling you since you were in kindergarten to shape up or ship out. Instead, look at you! You're just another nobody."

"I am a nobody with connections," Slim snarled. "Wait until my dad hears about this."

"Good," Carter said. "I'm looking forward to meeting him." Then he turned to the sheriff. "You sure you don't want to take me in, Sheriff? I'd be more than happy to sit in jail for a while."

The sheriff shook his head. "That's the last thing I need. His dad'll already be riled up that I'm locking up Slim."

"*More* than locking up," Carter said, his voice soft. "He sure as hell had better be charged with *at least* reckless endangerment and attempted manslaughter. You know yourself how dangerous that pincer move is."

"Not only is it dangerous," Hailey said from beside him, "but I'm also pretty sure a young woman already died the same way not too long ago. Maybe two years back? Wasn't she your girlfriend, Slim?"

Slim looked at her, and the color bleached from his skin.

"That was an accident. You're not pinning that on me."

"I wonder if we should believe him or not..." Hailey turned to the sheriff. "Maybe you should take another look at that case."

CHAPTER 12

H AILEY COULDN'T BELIEVE they had caught Slim in her office. Finally he had been caught in the act of doing something wrong. Now if only she was as sure he'd been working alone. After the sheriff left, they went back to do a quick sweep, found nothing thankfully, then changed the security codes and left. "I'll have a locksmith come in, just in case more copies of our office keys have been distributed to Andy and God knows who else."

Now, back at home, she was too keyed up to rest. She paced the kitchen. She wanted food, but she wasn't hungry. She wanted coffee but didn't need anything else to jack up her nerves. The dogs, Matzuka included were stretched out on the floor sleeping.

Finally Carter walked over and placed a shot of whiskey in front of her. "Drink up."

She glared at him. "Why the hell would I want a shot of whiskey? Are you trying to get me drunk?"

"If it will give me some answers, maybe."

She frowned, spoiling for a fight. "What the hell is that supposed to mean?" she snapped.

"Answers," he said. "Answers about why you're such a bitch to me all the time."

Instead of stepping back, she glared at him. "Except for today," she said.

"Yes, except for today, in a time of crisis. But every other time? I've been here a lot over the last fifteen years."

She shrugged. "So? We got off on the wrong foot."

"No," he said. "I think it's a lot more than that. I've talked with Gordon, and I also had an interesting conversation with an old lady on the street today."

"What? You're talking about me with the locals?" She wanted to put him in his place right here, but she was also curious and weary. "What did you talk about?"

"She told me that I was supposed to come back, marry you, and put you out of your misery."

Color and heat flashed up her skin. When it drained again, it left her pasty white and icy cold. "She must be joking," she said bluntly.

"I don't think she was," he said. "And I have a theory. A theory I have yet to test because I couldn't get past your prickles."

She glared at him and lifted her nose in the air. "I don't know what you're talking about."

He laughed and spun her around so she was leaning against the counter. Then he grabbed her chin. "Let's find out," he said in a low voice.

He lowered his head and kissed her with a force that soaked up every ounce of blood in her veins and sent it ricocheting around her body. Her whole body pulsated, from her toes to her forehead and then back out her lips. She wound her arms around his neck and kissed him fiercely. He made a half guttural sound and shifted his lips on hers for a moment, adjusting the two of them. Then he tucked her closer and kissed her back just as hard.

But she couldn't let this happen. Finally she managed to gain some semblance of control and pulled herself back. She stared up at him, her chest heaving, his gaze going to her rounded breasts as they shifted with every movement. She had already felt his physical reaction when their hips had locked together. "We're not doing this."

"Why not? According to that old lady, you've had a crush on me for years."

"A schoolgirl crush," she said with a wave of her hand. "I'm a woman now."

"Absolutely," he said. "So, what was this just now?"

"Stress," she announced, desperately telling her hormones to gain control of this situation before she did something she would regret.

He took a step back and eyed her from head to toe, then back up again. "So, in the spirit of healing," he said, "do you want some stress relief?"

He waggled his eyebrows at her, and she stared at him, but laughter bubbled up from inside her. Because, damn it, she really did want some of his brand of stress relief. She seriously did. She looked at him and struggled to keep the words in her mouth.

"Your choice," he said, "but I heard sex is supposed to be great for getting rid of stress."

She took a deep breath, intent on saying *Hell no*, but the words that came out were different. "Hell yes," she said. Then she clamped a hand over her mouth.

He laughed. "I like that answer."

She slowly lowered her hand. "For just right now. Not for tomorrow."

"*Right now*. I would take right now, as in right here on the countertop."

She shook her head. "This way." She had already opened the buttons to her shirt and then ripped it off as she raced up to her bedroom. Carter followed closely behind her. At the top of the stairs, she dropped her shirt on the newel post. By the time she went around the corner, she had her camisole off. She left it tossed over the railing. She shucked her jeans and her socks and turned around to stare at him in just her panties when they reached her bedroom door. She figured he could take those off himself.

Her breath caught in the back of her throat as she realized he stood nude in front of her. He was a beaten-up warrior but stood proudly with his body a little more damaged than she'd expected. She dared not show it though. She smiled up at him, motioning at his prosthetics. "Glad to see those things don't slow you down."

She could almost feel a tremor going through him. It looked like relief, and she thought she understood. But, when he scooped her up, tossed her on the bed, and came down above her, he burst out laughing.

"Sweetie, I've been wanting to chase you around this ranch for well over a decade, as soon as you became legal."

"Instead," she said, rolling over so she was on top, "you went and married that bitch."

He nodded, a shadow in his eyes. "Gordon told me not to, but Gordon didn't know I was lusting after his sister and not wanting to break up a friendship over something like that."

"It depends if it was just about doing the horizontal tango," she said. "But, right now, I really don't give a shit."

He laughed, his hand cupping her bare breasts. "You still have too many clothes on."

She shifted back and forth rubbing against his shaft and whispered, "I do, but sometimes maybe that feels pretty nice too."

"It does, but not today or right now. Not when I've wanted you for so long."

Suddenly she found herself flipped on her back, her panties ripped and tossed to the side and her legs spread wide. He placed himself by her entrance and looked at her. She nodded and said, "Absolutely."

He plunged deep and hard.

She arched her back and cried out, grabbing his hair. He started to ride, driving deeper, faster, and harder until she exploded in his arms, crying out the whole time. When she heard his own cry of release, and his body shuddered, she held him as he collapsed beside her.

"I always wondered if you'd be a screamer," he said.

She laughed. Then she opened her eyes so she could look directly into his. "Too damn bad you didn't find out a long time ago then, huh?"

He slipped his hand up behind her head and pulled her closer. "That's all right. I figure we'll just make up for all the lost time tonight," he whispered.

CARTER DIDN'T KNOW how many times they woke and found each other only to exhaust themselves and fall back into asleep again. When he finally woke up the next morning, his body was still humming, satiated, happy, and replete. His arms were wrapped around Hailey, who lay curled up against him, snoring gently. He loved how she was completely unconcerned about her physical body. She lay nude without covers, comfortable in her own skin. Thank God she hadn't made any instinctive grimace when first seeing his nude body. After his accident, he had worked hard at rehab to be the best he could be for anybody, and he was the best he could be for himself, but he didn't know if that was any good anymore.

When his wife had left him, Carter knew more than just one issue was involved with her defection, but it still struck a nerve. A nerve that went way deeper than where he had thought it would. It was such a sense of abandonment and feeling like he was so much less. But Hailey … Hailey hadn't even grimaced. And, for that, Carter wanted to hug and kiss her all over again. They talked about his injuries throughout the night, and she'd cried when she saw some of the scars on his body. Then, at one point, he had even taken off his prosthetic and showed her his stump. She had kissed the edge of it several times with tears in her eyes too. He tried to reassure her that he was fine now.

He appreciated how the long years of recovery looked a lot less important now and a lot more distant in his thoughts. There was something very specific and enlightening and just heartwarming about lying here with somebody who accepted him in his broken condition without expecting him to get any better. He knew that, as time went on, he would probably strengthen up some more muscles as he used them in different activities and that the prosthetics themselves were built in a way he knew he could probably improve a lot more too. He'd heard about a great designer in New Mexico, Badger's wife a while ago. Carter was working with her now, and she had a lot of ideas he was anxious to implement in his next prosthesis designs.

What he had was very decent already, and the designer had been surprised at the quality and flexibility of what he was currently using, but she thought she could do better. Carter had seen Geir's and all the rest of their prosthetics, and Carter had been pretty amazed. He had a running blade himself, which would have made life a lot easier these last couple days when Carter was out packing Gordon around and trying to track people down, but he wanted to appear as normal as possible.

It was an interesting thing what people did, whenever they saw he was handicapped. They immediately treated him differently, almost as if he were deaf, and they had to raise their voices to get him to hear. Nothing was wrong with his senses, but they didn't seem to recognize that. When he wore clothing that hid the bulk of his prosthetics, they didn't notice and so treated him the same as everyone else.

"What are you thinking about?" Hailey murmured, wrapping her arms around his.

"That I should have done this a long time ago."

"You should have," she whispered with a chuckle. "We could have saved ourselves a lot of years of anger."

"I kept thinking it wasn't the right thing to do because you were Gordon's sister."

"And I kept thinking you were ideal because he really liked you as a man."

"Meaning, Gordon didn't like your other boyfriends?"

"Most of the time, because," she said, "I think he was always comparing them to you."

"I doubt it. Gordon and I are friends, but we never discussed the fact that maybe we should become family. And he certainly never gave me permission to bed his sister."

"No, I'm not surprised, but that doesn't change the fact I think that's what he wanted too."

"Well, he was very careful not to mention it to me," he said, thinking about all the conversations they'd had over the years. He didn't remember Gordon ever mentioning that

Carter should hook up with his sister. At least not before this visit. "Maybe I was putting up barriers that said I wasn't interested. I don't know. I'd have to talk to Gordon about it. I was obviously interested. Any healthy male around you would be interested, but I didn't want to ruin my friendship with Gordon if you and I didn't work out."

"Understood," she said. Then she yawned and snuggled into his embrace. "Do we have to get up yet?"

"Not unless you want to. At least we know Gordon was awake and will survive. But we still have a lot of very loose threads to tie up to make life a little easier on us."

"What about Matzuka? It's kind of like we forgot about him."

At that, they heard a bark. Carter turned to look at the floor beside him. He chuckled and greeted the dog. Matzuka jumped in the middle of the bed. Laughing, Hailey rolled over to make room for him. Matzuka stretched out between the two of them. They gave him a good morning cuddle, and then he started to bark lightly again.

"I think that message is for you," Hailey said. "He wants to go out."

"Me?" he asked, but he was already sitting and putting the sock over his stump, then attaching his prosthetic. He stood. "Come on, Matzuka."

Hailey jumped off the bed and raced to the bedroom door, stopping him. "Don't you want some clothes on?" she teased.

He glanced down and rolled his eyes. "I guess. It's not like any neighbors are around though."

"Be modest for the deer," she said.

"Huh. I'd be surprised if you've got any deer around with the number of dogs here." Still, he put on his boxers and then his jeans, while the dog waited impatiently by the bedroom door. After that, he made his way downstairs and opened the door so Matzuka could go out, then went back into the kitchen and put on coffee. He stared out into the morning landscape. It was after six-thirty a.m., almost seven according to his watch, but he and Hailey were both tired after a very stressful day yesterday followed by not much sleep last night.

He focused his attention on Matzuka, watching him greet the other dogs and wander around. He seemed to like it here or at least enjoyed being outside again. Carter thought this would be a good place for the dog. But as for him? Carter didn't know. He was getting more confused by the minute because, although Hailey had said it was just for the night, she was anything but a one-night stand. And neither was he.

Especially when he found somebody who could accept him for who he was. He wasn't interested in losing her. Not now. Probably never had been. Something kept bringing him back here. Sure, his buddy was here, but that back-and-forth with Hailey he'd never quite understood until now. He hurt for the years where she must have hurt too, and he hadn't even been aware. He'd just blocked it out as not a possibility.

And to think he'd married the wrong person instead, when Hailey had been there, waiting. That dented his heart a little bit more. But then life was like that. He thought of all the disappointments he'd been through and the problems and the things he wished he could go back and redo differently, yet there was no way to do so. Life was a bit of a bitch that way. In the distance, he heard the phone ring and realized it was probably Hailey's. With any luck, she was talking to her brother.

When could Gordon come home? Carter walked to where he had set up his laptop, then he sat down and studied what was going on in the company's books. He quickly lost himself in numbers and almost missed it.

He went back and realized entries on one account had been changed multiple times. It was coded, so he wasn't sure whether the employees understood those specific codes or not, but, as Carter went back and looked at the old entries, it became obvious to him that the figures had been changed, dropping them down by over 500 percent. And it was Gordon's ranch accounts. Accessed unbeknownst by Hailey. He frowned and checked the file's history. It was a numbered account. That always made him suspicious. People had numbered accounts all the time, but not ones that had multiple changed entries.

And the numbers here were changed not just once but many times. He frowned at that, his mind thinking of all the reasons. Then there was the second account … Sure, rotten data entry was one reason but not with these repeated changes kind of thing going on. Unless someone was fudging numbers to fit what they were trying to make the accounts look like. He checked it out and realized it was supposedly a property management company. But then, where were they getting those revised figures from? Who entered them? And why?

When Carter took another closer look, this was from one of Phil's corporate accounts. Carter frowned and checked the others, but nothing suspicious was there. Writing down some of the details, he got up and called for Matzuka. Then he walked into the kitchen to pour two cups of coffee and went back to Hailey. She sat in bed, leaning against the headboard with a blanket pulled up to her chest, talking to Gordon.

"I'm fine, Gordon," she said. "I promise I'll get out, and I'll feed everybody. ... Yes, I know. I'm still in bed but sorry. Yesterday was a little stressful." She looked up when Carter came in and grinned at him impishly. "Yes, I slept just fine. ... Yes, I'll drag Carter out of bed to come and help me. ... No reason he shouldn't help," she snapped at something Gordon had said.

Carter just chuckled. He placed a coffee near Hailey's side of the bed, then walked to his side to put his coffee down and hopped back in, jeans and all. Matzuka, not wanting to be left out, lay down beside him. He put the information into an email and sent it to both Hailey and Gordon, knowing they'd get the notification on their phones when they got off. He planned to go over his findings when the conversations was done. Or maybe later depending on their time alone...

He gently stroked Matzuka, checking his healing wounds. He was still sore and tender, and definitely big scabs were evident on his side. Carter wondered if any vet had seen him since he went missing and gently ran a hand over the dog's tattoo mark. The poor boy. He'd been through a lot. He rolled over onto his side and placed an arm around Matzuka. The two of them lay like that, Matzuka quite content to be with Carter, and that was always important.

Carter wondered if Matzuka had bonded as quickly with the guy who had beaten him. Not from what Carter saw when Harold had walked Matzuka through town yesterday. Carter was sure about that. The dog had walked at the end of the leash, as far away as possible from Harold Longfellow. But even that might have been just so Matzuka could check out whatever newness was around him.

Carter wished he'd had a chance to see Matzuka in a natural surrounding where he wasn't primed to be an aggressive threat dog. That was not who he was meant to be. As he looked down at him, he just smiled and buried his face in his neck while scratching him. But suddenly Matzuka sat up. A growl rose from deep in his throat as he bolted from the room. Carter stood and followed. The dog had better instincts than he did. He also had better hearing.

Downstairs, Carter could see a vehicle coming. Matzuka stood at the door, growling. "Well, you don't like him, huh? I wonder why." He placed several fingers on top of the dog's head and gently stroked him. He didn't calm down.

As soon as the sheriff hopped out of his truck, Matzuka barked like crazy. Carter eyed the deputy by Raleigh's side. He didn't know the kid. Then, grabbing Matzuka by the scruff, he ordered him to calm down. He immediately stopped barking, but the soft and gentle growl at the back of the dog's throat was an interesting response. Lots of ranch dogs were around, but none of those were as aggressive as Matzuka was right now. He didn't like something.

Carter snapped onto Matzuka the collar and a leash he had gotten last night while in town, then brought him to the front porch. "Good morning, Sheriff," Carter said.

The sheriff nodded, the easy camaraderie and polite facade no longer evident after their last meeting. He shoved his hands on his hips and said, "Is that the dog? I've got another report that says you stole it."

Carter gave him a gentle smile. "*Stole?*"

"According to the report I got this morning, you walked across the street, had a few words with Harold, then grabbed the dog out of Harold's hand, took it back into your truck, and left."

"So he showed you a valid bill of sale, right?" Carter asked.

The sheriff simply frowned at him.

"As I already explained, this is the War Dog named Matzuka, who I came to find on behalf of US Navy Commander Cross from the War Dogs division," Carter said. "So, of course, your complainant signed an official police report. I hope he didn't commit perjury," Carter stated, staring down the sheriff. "And this witness produced valid documentation to supplement his police report, correct?"

The sheriff slid his gaze sideways to the man with him.

Carter turned toward the deputy, leaning over the hood of Gordon's truck. "Oh, look at this," Carter said. "Another Longfellow." He said it with such a sneer that the deputy immediately straightened.

"Hey, now," the sheriff said. "No need for that."

"Apparently there is. This town needs a bit of cleaning up."

"And you think," the deputy said, "you'll be man enough to do it? I don't think so, old man."

"David and Donnie and Brenda are getting on up there."

"They're the old ones," the deputy said. "That's what happens."

Something was in his tone, that casual lack of respect, that had Carter suddenly thinking something. He turned to the sheriff. "How old is Donnie?"

"In his eighties," the sheriff said.

"The woman I spoke to last night had to be a well-preserved lady in her late seventies or early eighties," Carter said.

"Brenda would fight it to her grave, but I'm sure she's over the eighty mark too." The sheriff pushed his hat back off his head slightly. "So?"

"And her husband, David?"

"Same. What are you getting at?"

Carter studied the deputy. The kid had to be in his early thirties or late twenties. "Sounds to me like the younger Longfellow generation doesn't want to wait until the older generation passes on naturally."

The deputy started to get irate. "You don't even know who I am."

"No, but I know you're related to Harold, the wannabe drug dealer in town, and you came here trying to defend him."

"We came here because you stole his dog."

"Show me that bill of sale that says it's his dog," Carter said. "Of course you came with it to show me, correct?"

"We'll have to see what the judge says in that case," the deputy said.

"Yes. Let's see the circuit court judge go up against the US Navy's War Dogs Division." Carter actually had no idea how much legal backing he had here, but it was a pretty good bluff.

The deputy frowned and looked at the sheriff, who just gave a one-arm shrug.

"I'm interested in seeing that too," Carter said, pointing to the sheriff, "since you're allowing Harold to continue to walk the streets and to take care of his illegal business practices. And yet when it comes to a War Dog that he was abusing and using to threaten people, you're not at all bothered."

"How do you know that?" The sheriff glared at Carter

now. "We've been getting reports of him having a dangerous dog many times."

"Of course. That's why you haven't done anything about it, correct? Here I thought maybe you were one of the good guys, Sheriff."

The sheriff continued glaring at Carter.

Carter nodded. "Yeah, I'm still here, and whoever shot Gordon is still out there. What have you done about that?"

Just then he heard footsteps behind him. He waited for Hailey to join him, now fully dressed by his side.

Hailey studied the deputy. "Walton, you're back to being a deputy again? I thought you lost your job." Then she turned to the sheriff. "Or was the pressure a little too much again, Sheriff? Must be tough to be between a rock and a hard place, between the law and the Longfellows."

"That's enough of that," Walton said, his voice harsh. "The sheriff's only doing what he's supposed to do."

"To stay elected, yes," she said quietly, "but not to uphold the law. So, what did you really come here about? Unless of course, you found Gordon's shooter? Or maybe you'll try and make that look like he did it himself too?"

"Maybe he did," Walton said. "I wouldn't put it past him to make it look like it was one of the Longfellows."

"Yeah, right," Carter butted in. "If it was a revolver maybe. But a 30-30 lever action? That's not happening."

"How do you know that?" Raleigh asked.

"Because I saw the bullet. And, if you were doing your job, you'd know where it came from yourself."

The sheriff pushed his hat back. "A lot of people have rifles out here."

"This was lever action, and he would have had to load it quickly in order to have fired two rounds," Carter said. "Or there were two shooters."

"Think you know a lot, don't you?" Walton asked. "But we're on the law side here, and it doesn't look like you're one of those law-abiding citizens who you keep talking about."

Carter waved a hand at him as if to tell him to shut up. He kept his gaze on the sheriff. "So, what'll it be, Sheriff? Are you even looking for Gordon's attacker?"

"Of course I am! I don't like you interfering in anything else."

"And yet you rehired Walton," Hailey said. "Back again, even after he beat up one of your suspects. Funny how that works. Do you really think we haven't already gone over your head and talked to the authorities in other counties to see what can be done about a bad sheriff here?"

"I'm not a bad sheriff."

"Maybe you're not fully there quite yet," Carter said. "Right now, you're on that knife's edge. Every day though, you have an opportunity to be the sheriff you should be or you can live up to the Longfellow reputation. And they'll take you down as soon as they have whatever it is they want from you."

"Since when did this become about Longfellows being bad guys?" Walton said, half-joking.

Carter deliberately ignored him.

That seemed to enrage him all the more. "Hey, you," Walton exclaimed. "You don't get to ignore me like that."

"Why not? You aren't saying anything I'm willing to listen to. You're not even supposed to be a deputy. You should have been fired from that position of trust a long time ago. So, the US government will have to open an investigation into that too. Your sorry ass should be in jail right now." Carter turned to Hailey. "Do you remember when it was?"

She nodded. "I also know who it was—somebody up against the Longfellows. They picked him up, took him to jail, and, while the sheriff here wasn't present, the deputies beat the crap out of him. He went to the hospital with several broken ribs. Those guys got sidelined until an investigation was done, but guess who's back at work now?"

"Since it happened in the jail cells, there should be videos of it. Aren't there, Sheriff?" Carter asked.

"That's our business," Walton said suddenly.

"Not anymore. I'll be sure to let the US government know what's going on in this county."

"He paid restitution," the sheriff said. "The victim's family decided not to press charges. I didn't have any choice."

"Hey," Walton said, "you don't get to tell him that."

The sheriff turned to him. "Shut up. You're only here as backup. I'm warning you, if you do that again, you're out of here."

"Whatever. Remember that your job's on the line too."

Raleigh shook his head. "It's not my job that's on the line. It's yours. Get back in that vehicle, and let me talk to them."

Walton shrugged and headed into the passenger seat of the truck.

"What's going on here?" Hailey asked as they walked into the kitchen.

"I'm under fire," the sheriff said, "and I'd appreciate it if you'd stop sending potshots my way. My job's tough enough right now. The Longfellows run this town, and the Longfellows make life difficult. The circuit court judge is also on their payroll."

"So much of the older generation is at an age where they

will soon be gone."

"There's a gap, yes. I'm not exactly sure how it started. A couple different accidents? The thirty-year-olds seem to be rumbling for power. We've still got the fifty to sixty-year-olds fighting them, like Manfred, but they're not winning. I think we'll have a real problem when the old ones pass on."

"I'm pretty sure that problem has already started," she said, "because this property dispute here was never a problem before, not while Donnie lived beside us for seventeen years."

The sheriff nodded. "Until Manfred moved in with his sons. Did you know Slim and Burgess are living over there too?"

"I didn't know that. That would explain a lot," Hailey said with a sigh. "What can we do? Obviously you're in trouble yourself."

Raleigh cast a glance where his deputy was seated. "It's a little worse than that. I think my office and the entire department is bugged."

At that, Hailey heard Carter suck in his breath. "Wow. That takes a lot of gall. Can you change the circuit judge or bring this up with somebody above you?"

"I've sent out a call for help," he said. "I'm waiting for a group to come down. The trouble is, it's not that easy."

"No, it's never that easy," Carter said. "But I will stop harassing you if we can see it's not a case of you being on the wrong side of the law. Because I won't tolerate that."

"I'm being slammed to the wall every day. I'm almost afraid my own house has been bugged."

"Speaking of bugs, we can check your offices," Carter said. "I had some equipment flown in."

The sheriff looked at him and narrowed his gaze. "Go ahead and check out mine tomorrow. If you find anything then we can check out my house. Discreetly, if you can. If I try to get that kind of equipment, it'll cause comments and further reactions."

"True enough," Carter said. "How many do we actually think might be involved in the takeover?"

"Like you mentioned earlier, I doubt it is the oldest Longfellow generation. Now that Fred is gone, we have the grandparents, the two brothers, Donnie and David Longfellow," the sheriff said, "and their three younger sisters, but one has passed on, one is battling cancer, while the third is pretty amicable. I don't think they're involved, but each of them has several daughters and sons. That middle generation doesn't worry me either. I think we're in trouble with the three grandsons."

"So, that's Slim, Walton, and who?" Carter asked. "Burgess?"

Raleigh shook his head. "He's an unsupervised teen. He's a problem, but he's his own separate problem. He's working alone."

"I agree. So Andy is the older grandson," Hailey said to Carter, but she faced the sheriff again. "We can't be sure that the women are completely out of this. But it is definitely a Slim and Walton kind of thing to do. Walton would get Donnie's farm because Donnie is his grandpa. Their father, Manfred, doesn't care about the land. Donnie hasn't been the same since his wife passed away."

"I think that's when Walton started to get too big for his britches," the sheriff said. Walton honked the horn in their vehicle, and the sheriff glared in that direction. "That's the kind of shit I have to put up with."

"What's the threat his father is holding over you?" Carter asked.

"Not his father," he said. "It's still Donnie, David, and Brenda who keep things in town peaceful. Fred played a huge peacekeeping part too, but he's gone now, so it's down to the other three. Not for long though, I think. Once they're gone, it falls to the next generation, but they aren't the immediate problem. These younger guys think they're big enough to take care of business themselves. And, in a way, they are, but they're rash and impulsive. They'll cross the line. There's a lot of brutality among them."

"Like the Burgess kid who beat up Diego's granddaughter," Carter said pointedly.

"If she'd come and talked to me, I could have done something about that. But she didn't." The sheriff glowered at Carter.

"Burgess isn't *already* on your radar?" Carter asked.

"Good Lord. He's just plain trouble but has always skirted the line."

"Yeah, he's a good decade-plus younger than Slim."

The sheriff nodded. "I can talk to Donnie and David. I'm not sure it'll do any good though."

"But they must have some hold on you," Carter repeated. "And that's the reason for all this."

"The hold is the fact that the Longfellows basically own the town, and they don't care if they just shut everything down, putting everybody out of work. We can't survive if that happens."

"The Longfellows own everything?"

"It seems like it," the sheriff said sadly. "What we need is some interjection of new money. We need the Longfellows to sell some of their business holdings so we can broaden the horizon of the town's ownership."

"What happens if you pick up all the grandsons and

charge them all with the crimes they've committed?"

"The three eldest Longfellows—David, Donnie, and Brenda—have said they would just shut everything down. I heard that a couple years ago, but I doubt they've changed their minds. They planned to close all businesses from one day to the next. They're old, so they don't care. They must have money saved, so don't need the property management income. They're dying eventually, and, if their grandkids aren't sticking around town, I don't think they'll consider the town necessarily something they want to keep fighting for."

Hailey shook her head. "We have to get to the middle generation because they're the ones who have to realize it's all their loved ones who will suffer."

"I know that," the sheriff said. "But, in the meantime, I need somebody who can give me a hand dealing with this. I need to bring in all five Longfellow boys, counting Burgess. He's nothing but a piece of shit. But I need to investigate that accusation by Diego and his granddaughter, but she doesn't want to talk. At the same time, I need to contact the middle generation and see if they'll do anything about the older generation's threat to shut down the town. I'm not sure Manfred and the rest of them have any more pull with the older generation than they do with the younger generation."

"How close is the older generation to making good on their threat?" Carter asked.

"I don't know," the sheriff said. "Too damn close as far as I know. I think these grandkids are all quite happy to have their protection right now, but ..."

"What does any of this have to do with Phil's and Fred's deaths?" Hailey interrupted.

Raleigh turned to look behind him and then lowered his

voice. "I heard Walton on the phone with Slim. It seems like they didn't know you would inherit the company."

She stared at him. "Who did they think would?"

"They thought their family would. Don't forget Fred. He's one of the old guys. He was the third brother—technically, he married into the family, so he was their brother-in-law. Anyway, Donnie and David Longfellow must have thought Fred's finance company would be left to the family—to Slim in particular."

"Why would that happen?" Hailey asked, frowning. "We have a partnership agreement that says otherwise."

"Because Fred apparently told Slim it would."

Hailey shook her head. "No, he wouldn't say that. But Slim might have dreamed up that fantasy."

"I don't know," the sheriff said, "but I'm pretty damn sure it's all related."

"Shit," Carter snapped. "Do you really think that generation is so bad that they killed Fred to get the company? Potentially killing Phil and Betty too?"

The sheriff took a deep breath, then slowly nodded. "The trouble is, all my deputies are Longfellows."

"WHEN ARE THE reinforcements coming in?"

"Later today," Raleigh said. "So, I'm more or less here to give you a warning. I need you guys to stay out of sight. Things could get bad."

Just then came a hard voice behind them. "What did you just say?"

Raleigh stiffened, then turned to see Walton by the doorway. "I told you to stay in the truck."

"You're not giving the orders here anymore, old man," Walton said. "I'm taking over as sheriff. Hand over your badge. You're done."

The sheriff shook his head. "Boy, you're so damn wet behind the ears you don't even know which way is up."

Walton pulled his weapon and pointed it at the sheriff. "Did you hear me?"

Matzuka stood outside on the porch, standing very still, waiting for the hand signal from Carter. Once received, Matzuka took one look at Walton, but, instead of jumping forward, he went right for his ankle and bit down hard. Then pulled up and back. The movement was so fast it sent Walton toppling forward and out of control. The sheriff lunged and grabbed the gun, then handcuffed Walton on the ground.

He swore from top to bottom while he did so. "Stupid damn kid," Raleigh said. "That's enough of that shit."

"You need to take a moment here," Hailey said quietly to the sheriff, "and find out who else is involved in this."

Carter turned to Walton. "What's this all about?"

Walton sneered at all of them before speaking to the sheriff. "It doesn't matter, old man. When you think you're safe, you won't be. We're all against you. Not one damn deputy in that department you can count on. Every one of them knows you're done."

"Thanks for that," the sheriff said quietly. He took the deputy badge off Walton's pocket and pinned it on Carter's pocket. "You're now deputized, whether you like it or not."

Walton started cussing. "You can't do that. We'll take him out in the back alley and pop him one if you do this."

"Just like you did Phil and his wife?" Hailey asked.

"Old Phil and his wife were pieces of shit. They were

supposed to leave all their shares to their foster daughter," he said. "Instead it all went to this Hailey bitch. Like, what kind of bullshit is that? Family first."

Hailey gasped. "Angela? Your ex-girlfriend?"

"She's not really my ex as we never broke up," he said. "We've been seeing each other steadily since we got together the first time."

"And the only reason you stayed friendly with her was because you thought she would get all those shares of the company? And then what? You'd marry her and kill her?"

He shrugged. "If that is the fastest way to move up in life, sure. I have no problem with that."

"Is that how the old ones did it? Donnie, David, and Fred—is that what they did?" Carter asked, his voice harsh. "Step on everyone and take out the ones in their way, then just buy up whatever was left for pennies?"

"Sure, that's what they all did—it was the way back then. Fred just became soft in his old age. Comes from not having a family of his own. And then all our parents got soft. They like the easy life. They just sat there and ran a bunch of businesses and lived off the income. No expectations of getting bigger. They were more than happy to start selling their stores so they had less to look after. Which just means less income for us. Like, how will that be of any benefit to me?"

"I see," Carter said. "So, instead of letting your parents retire—did you know that's what old folks do? They actually retire—you were all about looking at where your future money would come from. But not from a job of course."

"Of course I was expecting money from them," Walton said with half a gasp. "What do you think I am, a fool? Of course I'm looking after myself. That's all anybody ever looks after." Walton shook his shoulders and his handcuffed hands, then smiled. "Don't worry. This is nothing because I'll be out of these in no time. Dear Grandpa will fix this."

"I wonder," the sheriff said. "We'll have to put it to the test, won't we?"

CHAPTER 13

HAILEY WATCHED AS the sheriff and Carter loaded Walton up into his truck. Carter, in his own vehicle, with Matzuka in the front passenger seat, took off behind the sheriff. Now Hailey was stuck at home doing a ton of ranch chores, but she also needed to get to the hospital to talk to her brother. The email Carter had sent her was a bombshell. She was still processing the information. That the creative bookkeeping was someone from her own company defied belief. She needed to talk to Gordon about the mess too. She pulled out her phone and called Debbie. "How's Gordon?" Hailey asked.

"He's sleeping again," she said. "I've got a cot in here now. I'll stay beside him the whole time."

"Are you guys okay?"

"Yes," Debbie answered in a happy voice. "We are."

"Good," Hailey said, "but look. Shit's happening down here. I'll run out and do the chores, and then I'm not sure what my next job is." She filled in Debbie on what had happened with Walton and the sheriff. Then what Carter's next plan entailed.

"What?" Debbie cried out. "Seriously, can you do that?"

"Obviously we've got a Longfellow uprising coming, and the sheriff is about to be deposed, and we need to stop whatever we can."

"Carter has been deputized now?" Debbie said with a note of amusement. "You know what? That's a perfect job for him."

"I don't know about that," Hailey said. "He seems to be pretty damn good at a lot of things. He's helping me find whoever has been cheating the company. I think it's Andy and Slim together. Maybe more of them, I'm not sure yet. According to what Carter found one account is missing sixty grand and our ranch accounts were devalued. As if a takeover was going to be attempted."

"Oh, my gosh, I didn't know about that either," Debbie said. "You didn't tell me."

"I haven't exactly had time," Hailey said. "We're still working on some of it."

"But somebody has definitely been embezzling from the company?"

"Let's say, they've been fixing the books and making it look like things have done better than they have—or done worse, as the case may be. And maybe it's to inflate the company's worth too. I don't know how far back this has gone, but I've got to get to the bottom of it. It won't be easy."

"Are you keeping the company?"

"According to Walton, Phil's portion was supposed to go to his foster daughter, Angela."

"But I thought you said it wasn't. It was supposed to go to the other partners."

"Yeah, the partners all signed contracts to that end. But maybe Angela was under the impression she would get it because she was the only family Phil had."

"Well, good thoughts and all that …"

"Exactly," Hailey said. "According to the lawyers, the

company's mine. But I've got a hell of a mess to clean up. A lot of hard feelings and a lot of suspicious looks. I'm sure an awful lot of bad attitudes go with the rest. So, it'll be fun getting it straightened out." Then Hailey paused. "But, right now, I have to make sure the ranch is safe and everybody's fed. And I need to watch my back. I'm all alone here, except for one volunteer cop who has been watching the disputed fence line. The ranch hands are out in the pastures. I have no way to contact him so I'm not sure if he's even still here. Anyway, I just wanted to make sure you weren't heading home, and you were staying with Gordon."

"Don't you worry," Debbie said, her voice firm. "We've still got a cop on guard duty here too. Nobody will get to Gordon again. He'll have to go through that officer *and* me."

"That's what I'm warning you about," Hailey said. She dropped her voice. "They *will* go through you to get to him. So please be on guard and don't get hurt."

Then she hung up. As soon as she did, she loaded her two shotguns she kept on the ranch and in her bedroom, separate from Gordon's stash locked in the front room. Just in case she couldn't get to those when needed. Then, carrying one of them outside, the ranch dogs accompanying her, she checked on the other animals. There were always chores when you ran a ranch. No days off. She never shirked her part of it, but she left the Monday-to-Friday stuff to Gordon because she had to work in town. The amount of work that needed to be done on a daily basis at the ranch was always hours' worth.

As soon as she was done with the regular chores, she walked over to Smokey, her appaloosa gelding, and hopped on. With the shotgun riding across her knees, she took a slow and careful walk through the pastures, some of the ranch dogs coming along. From where she stood, hidden in the copse, she could see where they had found Gordon's body. No sign of anyone was around, and the dogs didn't appear to be too concerned with anything either.

The only difference between now and then was she wasn't out in the open, and Gordon had been. The shooter had been in the trees where she was now. She slowly surveyed the area, but she found nothing here. Turning the horse around, she cantered most of the way home. After that, she took off the halter and the saddle, brushed Smokey, gave him a few oats and a slap on the neck, then headed toward the house.

She had had no phone calls since the sheriff's visit. At the porch, she was wondering about him and Carter as she took the first couple steps, then tripped on the next step, slamming her knee into the next riser. When the wood splintered beside her head, she dove inside the doorway, dragging the shotgun with her. She swore softly and then stopped. That was close. The wood had splintered right beside her.

The dogs came crowding in after her, and she managed to slam the door just as they got in. Then she sat inside, her back against the front door. Now she swore out loud as she phoned Carter. He answered on the first ring. "Somebody's shooting at me at the ranch. Almost caught me too," she said.

This time it was his turn to swear. "We're about ten minutes out. Make sure you stay alive until I get there."

She laughed. "Why? I've been here the whole time, and you didn't give a shit then."

"It's different now," he said tersely. "Don't make me come in there and smack you for that."

"Could be fun," she said, chuckling. Just then a window shattered, and glass rained all over her. "Goddamn it. That window cost several hundred bucks."

"I want you to stay away from the windows too. Do I have to tell you that again?"

"I'm on the ground in front of the double oak doors, but I can't see anything."

"Don't even try to."

"Yeah, and what'll stop the shooter from coming up the front steps and in the front door? He at least shot at the window, so now I've got a way to shoot back at him." She lowered her voice. It almost sounded like she growled out the next words. "And you better believe I will shoot without mercy. The minute there's a footfall on that step, I'm pulling the trigger on the shotgun."

"That's my girl," Carter said. "But try not to engage them until I get there. You stay alive and away from a confrontation like this, okay? Once you start a gunfight, nobody wins."

"I hear you, but, in this case, something major has to blow up before we'll get this to stop."

"We've got both Slim and Walton in jail," he said. "We still have to pick up Andy and Harold. Apparently, all four of them are in it together. Burgess is on the list too, but he was acting out on his own."

"What about the talk with the elders?" Hailey asked.

"We had a talk with the middle generation. None of them believe it, and they're all sure we're mistaken. Donnie and Brenda are suspiciously silent. David's in the hospital."

"What's wrong with David?"

"A heart attack," Carter said. "Last night."

"I'm betting Slim and Walton brought that on."

"We think so too. I think it's also why Brenda and Donnie are quiet. There's definitely an ongoing power struggle."

"If you've got two of the assholes down, then I've got the other two here at the ranch. But one's just an asshole, and one's a wannabe drug dealer," Hailey said. "Too bad you didn't leave Matzuka here."

"I'm about to let him out at the gate. I'm coming down the driveway."

"So, why are you letting the dog loose?"

"Because he's a whole lot smaller and harder to hit. They won't be expecting it. When they see the truck, they'll start firing as soon as I get within range."

"Only once," she said. "Only once." Then she hung up. Calling the dogs to her, keeping them quiet and out of the way was paramount. Matzuka might be trained for conflict but the others weren't. Yet they would defend her if that's what the fight came too.

She studied the living room, looking for a way to get a better view as to who and what was coming toward her. On her hands and knees, she crawled carefully under the broken window and around to the other side, then carried on underneath the second set of windows where a partial room divider of logs was. There, she stood on the other side of it and peered through the windows.

The two guys were at the barn, one on either side. Why were they attacking her? Was it because of the sheriff warning her earlier? Or because she was the one stopping them from getting the company? Although how they figured they'd get it now, she didn't know. The lawyer had already drawn up the paperwork. In the case of her death, the company went to her brother and to Carter, even though

Carter didn't know about it. Were the Longfellow grandsons planning on taking out her and Gordon, so they could take over their ranch then? Because that wouldn't work either. If so, they were plenty stupid enough to think they could do that and then get away with murdering her and her brother.

Another bullet fired harmlessly at the front door. She just watched and waited because what the shooters didn't know was they would soon get ambushed from behind the barn. She watched as Carter's truck came into view alongside the sheriff's. Instead of coming down the road and raising a cloud of dirt, they carefully drove across the field. As she watched, it looked like they shut off the engines, coasting now, and just rolled up behind the barn. From the far side, she could see Matzuka racing toward one side of the barn too.

She heard a sharp whistle, then looked to where Carter was. With Matzuka now at his side, Carter and Raleigh split up and went around the barn. Hailey raised the shotgun, afraid she wouldn't be in time to save either man because all it would take was for these two idiots to turn around and take out both men. The younger idiot, suddenly hearing something, turned and fired. He fired again and again, but she saw his gun fly in the air, a shot going wild. Matzuka had charged him and jumped to lock his jaw on the man's shoulder. Screaming, Andy stumbled backward and went down under the dog's charge, ending flat on his back.

"Matzuka, release," Carter ordered, his voice easily reaching her at the house.

But Matzuka wasn't having any of it. He growled and shook the sobbing man's shoulder. Finally, getting him calmed down, Carter ordered Matzuka to release his prey again.

This time Matzuka released his grip on the man now unconscious on the ground, then sat and stood guard over Andy. Carter stood over the man his dog had knocked out cold.

However, as Carter was preoccupied moving the unconscious man, Harold stepped in behind him and raised his gun and held it against Carter's head.

She watched it happen, her throat closing in fear as the tables suddenly turned. It was almost like a comical movie, but nothing was funny about it. She couldn't hear the words spoken between the two men, but she could imagine …

And just when she thought all was lost, the sheriff came up behind, and he put his gun against Harold's back. Hailey exhaled the breath she didn't realize she held. She shook her head and pushed open the door.

"Just in case you think he's alone," Hailey called out, motioning behind Harold with her raised shotgun pointing at him too, "he's not alone at all."

The wannabe drug dealer turned and glared at her.

She shrugged. "At least you should realize when you're beaten. Now, get on the ground, beside your asshole cousin there."

With no other choice, he dropped to the ground. Just then, a shot came from around the side of the house. It narrowly missed Hailey. She stepped behind the railing where there was nothing to be seen, but still she raced toward the shooter, even though she heard Carter swear at her to run away. But, with the sheriff holding his gun on Harold, Carter needed to secure the two men they had down, so she had to be the one to act. She went around and came up against somebody else with a gun.

"Well, look at that—Angela, Phil's errant foster daughter. Did you really think the company was Phil's to hand off like that?" Hailey asked.

Angela stared at her with glowing animosity. "Of course it was. I'm his only family."

"You mean, you're his only family now?"

"Yes, so it's all mine. As is his house and other property. He told me that I would inherit it all."

"I don't think so anymore. I think you'll find he mortgaged it to pay for his medical care."

"No way. They had lots of money."

"But lots more in medical expenses," Hailey said gently. "It's one of the reasons Phil was still working well past the point he hoped he needed to. Did you have to kill both of them?"

Angela shrugged. "Who gives a shit? The old lady was just about as dead as Phil was anyway."

"If you'd waited a little longer, she would have died on her own. Then you wouldn't be up on three murder charges."

Hailey still held the shotgun while the other woman held her small revolver. They were definitely at a stalemate. Hailey could shoot Angela and blast her into shreds, but Hailey would likely take a bullet at these close quarters too.

Where was Matzuka? Hailey tried to look around but didn't dare take her eyes off the greedy heartless young woman in front of her.

"We took them both out because I would inherit everything. Why wait for him to spend more? Phil had one foot in the grave already. Talk about a waste of money."

The coldness of her words momentarily stopped Hailey in her tracks. So much entitlement and hatred. Such a lack of love. ... Did Angela have any compassion for what that couple went through? "What about poor Fred? Did he deserve to get shot too?"

"Yes," Angela cried out. "What's with all these old folks sticking around and not dying in time for the younger generation to actually get anywhere? You think we want to sit here and wait until they finally kick the bucket?"

"You could try that," Hailey said. "You forget another generation stands in the middle."

"Yeah," Angela said, "but they're useless. They're too soft, too easy, and they've been puppets for a long time. The older generation was dominant. And they made the next generation weak." Then she chuckled. "But that's all right because a strong generation is back again. We don't even have to take out the middle generation. We'll just step into place. Pretty damn easy. They haven't given us any resistance yet."

"I think that's because they didn't realize what you were doing," Hailey said. "So, yes, maybe they were blind. And maybe they also weren't thinking their beloved children would do something like this. I wonder what they'll do when they find out you killed some of their parents."

Angela shrugged. "Whatever."

"And Fred. You killed Fred for what? Because you five thought one of you could get his part of the company?"

"Fred told Slim that he was getting it. I was to get Phil's portion and he was getting Fred's. We were going to have Andy cook the books to inflate the value then sell it off. Andy has been embezzling money for all of us for a couple of years now. But he can't get caught so we'll sell in the chaos following the multiple partner deaths. And we'll live just ..." She sneered. "Believe me, while the lawyers have this all tied up, you'll be bankrupt along with the rest of them."

Behind Angela, Hailey could see Matzuka and Carter approaching. Relief that the stalemate was about to end but nervous that everything could still go wrong, she kept Angela focused on her. "Oh, I don't think so, but that's all right. I'll see you in court. Of course you and your buddies will be coming with a public defender from behind bars after murdering three people."

Angela laughed. "No one can prove I had anything to do with this."

"Says you," Hailey said cheerfully. "You're all going down for three murders along with all the other related charges."

Just like that though, Angela lifted the revolver and aimed. "I'll just end it all by fucking shooting you. I don't care."

Matzuka howled deep in his throat, ... a sound guaranteed to fill anyone's veins with ice. And he was right behind Angela.

"Shit," Angela whispered as she glanced wildly from side to side.

"I wouldn't pull that trigger if I were you," Hailey said gently. "Matzuka's a little unhappy right now."

Angela's shaky fingers were ready to pull the trigger, but the sound of the gun cocking came from behind her too. She froze and glared at Hailey. "Who the hell else could be around here? Aren't there fucking enough of you guys already? And to take over Harold's dog—that's just wrong ..."

"I think that's our line," Carter said from behind Angela. He held the gun right at her head. "Give me an excuse to blow your head to smithereens, but, if you want to live another day, you'll take that gun, and you'll drop it on the ground."

She hesitated.

"Or I can order Matzuka to attack, and he can tear apart your shoulder so your right arm will hurt like hell for the rest of your lazy ill-gotten life."

She glared at Hailey who still stood in front of her.

Hailey could see Angela considering her options, until Matzuka growled one high-pitched eager sound that had Angela hastily throwing her weapon off to the side. "That's all right. We've got money and lawyers. You'll never lock us up."

Carter laughed. "Raleigh's getting ready to lock up the lot of you. And you don't have money anymore. It seems to have been fabricated from thin air."

"What the hell?" Angela yelled, turning to face Carter.

"Yep, your man Andy cooked the book with his creative accounting. Although trying to make Hailey and Gordon's ranch broke was beneath you. Still his numbers are all hocus pocus. And those lawyers you talk about?"

Angela frowned.

"They'll probably be disbarred for what they've helped the Longfellows do for decades to this town. So, like Hailey said, you and the other four will probably have to share one public defender. Good luck with that."

Finally Hailey could feel the tension draining off her shoulders.

Carter ignored Angela for the moment and focused on Hailey. "Are you okay?"

"I sure am," she said. "This little witch turned out to be part of the murders. Oh, and, Angela, our ranch was never put up as collateral against my company buy-in. So not sure why devaluing my ranch on crooked books would help you there. It's paid for as is the company—my company not yours. And I have enough legal documents to make sure that never becomes a legal challenge. And if you kill me, Carter here inherits it all with my brother. Between Andy and Slim, with your agreement with the murders, the pincer move on the road to take me out, shooting my brother... all of it should put you and the others away for a lifetime."

Angela stared at her, all the color fading from her skin.

Carter stepped up to her side. "At least that long." He smiled at Angela. "Let's go."

"You can tell the sheriff whatever you want," Angela said. "I'll just deny it. You two are fucking nuts anyway, so nobody'll listen to you."

"Well, that would be true, except for this." Carter held up his phone and replayed the recording from the beginning. It was enough to recognize Angela's sneering voice talking about Fred's, Phil's, and Betty's deaths.

Angela's eyes widened, and she swore.

After that, Carter led Angela to where the other two lay on the ground. While all three were now on the ground, facedown, Carter played the tape for the sheriff.

Raleigh shook his head in disgust. "Good Lord."

"Now what about your deputies?" Carter asked.

"The other team came in. They are back at the station," the sheriff said. "The other two deputies are under house arrest until we can interrogate them. As for Walton, after what he did today before my very eyes, and according to this recording, it'll be a long time before he ever sees daylight again." Then he paused and looked at Carter and Hailey. "I know you want to stay here, but ..."

"Go," Hailey said to Carter, smiling. "These guys need to be in jail. And I want to make sure the sheriff is safe too."

Carter looked at her and frowned.

"Go," she said.

He reached over and kissed her hard. "Make sure you're here when I get back."

She batted her eyelashes. "We'll have a day or two before Gordon comes home from the hospital, so you better get home fast."

The sheriff sighed. "Could you two just keep all that mushy stuff for later? We have business to attend to."

Carter chuckled before reaching out to grab the two men. He helped them to their feet and led them to the sheriff's vehicle. Then he shoved them both into the back seat, while Raleigh put Angela in with them. Carter turned to look at Hailey. "Do you want to follow us in the ranch truck? I'll ride in with the sheriff to make sure nobody plays any games." He didn't wait for her answer though. He picked up the multitude of weapons they'd confiscated and stowed them in the floorboard before Carter climbed into the passenger seat up front in the sheriff's dual-cab truck.

Hailey smiled. That was a good idea. She opened the passenger door of Gordon's truck, then called for Matzuka. Matzuka came along with Bonnie and Clyde, Hailey's two border collies. All three dogs rode in the front seat as she headed out behind the sheriff and Carter. She smiled as she drove.

Debbie called her a few moments later and said, "Did you hear anything?"

She laughed and updated her sister-in-law. "Yeah, it's over. It was the younger generation. All five of them."

"Oh, my word," Debbie cried out. "To think all that happened while we were here."

"Yeah, we're taking them to jail to make sure nobody

else gets loose," Hailey said. "And then I'm going home, and I'm bringing Carter with me. We're going to bed, and we're not leaving for days. Do you hear me?"

At that, Debbie laughed a hearty belly laugh. "So, does that mean Gordon has to stay in the hospital a little longer?"

"Keep him there for a week or two," Hailey said humorously. "Carter and I have a lot of time to make up for."

"I'm seriously thrilled for you," Debbie said warmly. "I know this is what you've wanted for a long time."

"I have. I just don't know how to make him stay."

"There's nothing to *make*," Debbie said. "It's what he always wanted as well. He was just too scared he might ruin his friendship with Gordon."

Hailey stared at the phone. "You know what? That's exactly what Carter told me earlier, but I didn't believe him."

"That's too bad," Debbie said, "because it's true. Now, go enjoy your future."

"Oh, I plan on it. You take care of Gordon for me."

"Done deal."

EPILOGUE

WESTON THURLOW WALKED into the offices of the Titanium Corp, then threw himself down into a chair, and said, "I want in."

Cade gave him a blank stare.

Then Erick, who was between the two of them, looked at Weston and asked, "Want in what?"

"Whatever deal it is all these guys are disappearing into."

Erick looked at Cade, and they both turned to look at Weston. "Say what?" both asked at the same time.

"Oh, no, no," Weston said. "I've heard all kinds of stuff, so no holding back on me."

"All kinds of *what* stuff?"

"Pierce, Blaze, Zane, Parker, Lucas, and even Ethan," he said. "What the heck's going on with that? I heard something about dogs recently."

"Why? Are you interested in dogs?" Erick asked.

Just then Geir walked in. "What was that about dogs?" he asked, before tossing a file in front of them. Attached to the front of it was a picture of Carter, leaning on a fence railing, a woman's arms wrapped around him, their faces pressed together. They both looked deliriously happy.

Cade looked at it and grinned. "Another one bites the dust," he said.

"Or we could say, *Another very successful story*," Erick

corrected, nudging him with his shoulder.

Cade nodded. "Or we could say, *They look happy together.*"

"Don't they?" Weston hopped up and walked around to take a look. "Yeah, that's Carter. What the hell has he been up to? And who's the woman?"

"Sister of his best friend," Geir said. "He needed to go back and fix a few things. And found where his heart really lay."

"Oh, all that touchy-feely stuff," Weston said, his face scrunching up. "But what kind of jobs are they doing? Do you know how boring it is to sit here day in and day out? All I do is build homes in the daytime and play my music at night."

"And yet here you are, looking for another job," Cade said.

Weston shrugged. "Yeah, because I'm bored. Don't you have something better for me to do?"

"Do you have any experience with dogs?"

"Some. I worked in a K9 unit for a while."

"Only a while?"

"I got promoted," he said. "Then I got blown up. You know how that works. Life takes you down a path you didn't expect to go." And, of course, he knew they did know. They had all been down a path nobody had been prepared for.

Geir smiled at him. "What part of the country are you from?"

"Why?"

"Because we've got dogs all across the country, and we're trying to fit people who have a reason to go someplace to track down these dogs. I have little-to-no budget money for this." He quickly explained about the defunct War Dogs program.

Weston's gaze narrowed with interest; then he grinned. "Wow. Sounds like a real mess."

"Yep, that's exactly what it is. But we have seven down and five more to go."

"Did they all come to the mainland?"

"You mean, in the US?"

He nodded. "Yeah, that's what I'm asking."

"One's in Alaska, and one's in Hawaii. Does that count?"

Weston jumped up. "I'll take the one in Alaska. It would be Anchorage, right?"

"That's where it was flown to. But I think it went out to a homestead family."

"Good," he said. "I'm from Alaska, and I've been looking to go back for a visit."

"Did you leave a long-lost love back there too?"

He winced. "Not exactly."

"What does that mean?"

"I left a little daughter back there," he said, "adopted out to a very nice family. Only I know the family lost the husband recently. That was a year ago maybe? And they've been asking me if I could stop by for a visit because my little girl wants to get to know her biological dad now that her other dad's gone."

All the men looked at him in surprise.

"I know," he said. "I didn't exactly expect to have a child. But, when my one-night stand ended up telling me a year afterward that she'd had a child and put it up for adoption, yeah, you could say it wasn't exactly a crowning moment of my life."

"We don't pay, but there are plenty of benefits."

"It doesn't matter," Weston said, his face drawn. "It's definitely time to face the music."

"Good," Geir said. "Because the dog in Alaska? Her name is Shambhala, and she could really use a music lover."

"Why is that?"

"Because she's blind in one eye, and she limps. But she's got excellent hearing, and she loves to listen to music." Geir reached through the stack and checked the folders. Then he pulled out one and handed it to Weston. "You get a copy of that and not a whole lot else."

Weston grinned. "I'll take it."

This concludes Book 7 of The K9 Files: Carter.

Read about Weston: The K9 Files, Book 8

THE K9 FILES: WESTON (BOOK #8)

Welcome to the all new K9 Files series reconnecting readers with the unforgettable men from SEALs of Steel in a new series of action packed, page turning romantic suspense that fans have come to expect from USA TODAY Bestselling author Dale Mayer. Pssst... you'll meet other favorite characters from SEALs of Honor and Heroes for Hire too!

Weston was at an impasse in his life, after hearing about his unknown daughter, who'd already been adopted by another family. Only the father had since passed away... So ... accepting the mission to track down the missing, blind-in-one-eye, limping K9 dog named Shambhala—in Alaska—was exactly where he needed to be to sort out this other issue in his life. Finding the dog turned out to be easier than Weston had expected, but sorting out how and why this dog's owners had been murdered was something else again.

Now a widow, Daniela knew her daughter also needed a father, so she'd contacted Weston, not sure if he even knew of the baby's existence. When he said he was on the way, she was concerned at what she'd started and that emotion then turned to terror when Sari's birth mother showed up at Daniela's doorstep, looking for her daughter again.

Things turn ugly when Weston's K9 investigation impacts his daughter's life and her new mother. He must do something, or everything he's finally found will be lost.

Find Book 8 here!
To find out more visit Dale Mayer's website.
http://smarturl.it/DMSWeston

Author's Note

Thank you for reading Carter: The K9 Files, Book 7! If you enjoyed the book, please take a moment and leave a short review.

Dear reader,

I love to hear from readers, and you can contact me at my website: www.dalemayer.com or at my Facebook author page. To be informed of new releases and special offers, sign up for my newsletter or follow me on BookBub. And if you are interested in joining Dale Mayer's Reader Group, here is the Facebook sign up page.
https://smarturl.it/DaleMayerFBGroup

Cheers,
Dale Mayer

Get THREE Free Books Now!

Have you met the SEALS of Honor?

SEALs of Honor Books 1, 2, and 3. Follow the stories of brave, badass warriors who serve their country with honor and love their women to the limits of life and death.

Read Mason, Hawk, and Dane right now for FREE.

Go here and tell me where to send them!
http://smarturl.it/EthanBofB

About the Author

Dale Mayer is a USA Today bestselling author best known for her Psychic Visions and Family Blood Ties series. Her contemporary romances are raw and full of passion and emotion (Second Chances, SKIN), her thrillers will keep you guessing (By Death series), and her romantic comedies will keep you giggling (It's a Dog's Life and Charmin Marvin Romantic Comedy series).

She honors the stories that come to her – and some of them are crazy and break all the rules and cross multiple genres!

To go with her fiction, she also writes nonfiction in many different fields with books available on resume writing, companion gardening and the US mortgage system. She has recently published her Career Essentials Series. All her books are available in print and ebook format.

Connect with Dale Mayer Online

Dale's Website – www.dalemayer.com
Facebook Personal – https://smarturl.it/DaleMayer
Instagram – https://smarturl.it/DaleMayerInstagram
BookBub – https://smarturl.it/DaleMayerBookbub
Facebook Fan Page – https://smarturl.it/DaleMayerFBFanPage
Goodreads – https://smarturl.it/DaleMayerGoodreads

Also by Dale Mayer

Published Adult Books:

Hathaway House
Aaron, Book 1
Brock, Book 2
Cole, Book 3
Denton, Book 4
Elliot, Book 5
Finn, Book 6
Gregory, Book 7
Heath, Book 8
Iain, Book 9

The K9 Files
Ethan, Book 1
Pierce, Book 2
Zane, Book 3
Blaze, Book 4
Lucas, Book 5
Parker, Book 6
Carter, Book 7
Weston, Book 8

Lovely Lethal Gardens
Arsenic in the Azaleas, Book 1
Bones in the Begonias, Book 2

Corpse in the Carnations, Book 3
Daggers in the Dahlias, Book 4
Evidence in the Echinacea, Book 5
Footprints in the Ferns, Book 6
Gun in the Gardenias, Book 7
Handcuffs in the Heather, Book 8
Ice Pick in the Ivy, Book 9

Psychic Vision Series
Tuesday's Child
Hide 'n Go Seek
Maddy's Floor
Garden of Sorrow
Knock Knock...
Rare Find
Eyes to the Soul
Now You See Her
Shattered
Into the Abyss
Seeds of Malice
Eye of the Falcon
Itsy-Bitsy Spider
Unmasked
Deep Beneath
From the Ashes
Stroke of Death
Psychic Visions Books 1–3
Psychic Visions Books 4–6
Psychic Visions Books 7–9

By Death Series
Touched by Death

Haunted by Death
Chilled by Death
By Death Books 1–3

Broken Protocols – Romantic Comedy Series
Cat's Meow
Cat's Pajamas
Cat's Cradle
Cat's Claus
Broken Protocols 1-4

Broken and... Mending
Skin
Scars
Scales (of Justice)
Broken but... Mending 1-3

Glory
Genesis
Tori
Celeste
Glory Trilogy

Biker Blues
Morgan: Biker Blues, Volume 1
Cash: Biker Blues, Volume 2

SEALs of Honor
Mason: SEALs of Honor, Book 1
Hawk: SEALs of Honor, Book 2
Dane: SEALs of Honor, Book 3
Swede: SEALs of Honor, Book 4
Shadow: SEALs of Honor, Book 5

Cooper: SEALs of Honor, Book 6

Markus: SEALs of Honor, Book 7

Evan: SEALs of Honor, Book 8

Mason's Wish: SEALs of Honor, Book 9

Chase: SEALs of Honor, Book 10

Brett: SEALs of Honor, Book 11

Devlin: SEALs of Honor, Book 12

Easton: SEALs of Honor, Book 13

Ryder: SEALs of Honor, Book 14

Macklin: SEALs of Honor, Book 15

Corey: SEALs of Honor, Book 16

Warrick: SEALs of Honor, Book 17

Tanner: SEALs of Honor, Book 18

Jackson: SEALs of Honor, Book 19

Kanen: SEALs of Honor, Book 20

Nelson: SEALs of Honor, Book 21

Taylor: SEALs of Honor, Book 22

Colton: SEALs of Honor, Book 23

Troy: SEALs of Honor, Book 24

SEALs of Honor, Books 1–3

SEALs of Honor, Books 4–6

SEALs of Honor, Books 7–10

SEALs of Honor, Books 11–13

SEALs of Honor, Books 14–16

SEALs of Honor, Books 17–19

Heroes for Hire

Levi's Legend: Heroes for Hire, Book 1

Stone's Surrender: Heroes for Hire, Book 2

Merk's Mistake: Heroes for Hire, Book 3

Rhodes's Reward: Heroes for Hire, Book 4

Flynn's Firecracker: Heroes for Hire, Book 5

Logan's Light: Heroes for Hire, Book 6
Harrison's Heart: Heroes for Hire, Book 7
Saul's Sweetheart: Heroes for Hire, Book 8
Dakota's Delight: Heroes for Hire, Book 9
Michael's Mercy (Part of Sleeper SEAL Series)
Tyson's Treasure: Heroes for Hire, Book 10
Jace's Jewel: Heroes for Hire, Book 11
Rory's Rose: Heroes for Hire, Book 12
Brandon's Bliss: Heroes for Hire, Book 13
Liam's Lily: Heroes for Hire, Book 14
North's Nikki: Heroes for Hire, Book 15
Anders's Angel: Heroes for Hire, Book 16
Reyes's Raina: Heroes for Hire, Book 17
Dezi's Diamond: Heroes for Hire, Book 18
Vince's Vixen: Heroes for Hire, Book 19
Ice's Icing: Heroes for Hire, Book 20
Johan's Joy: Heroes for Hire, Book 21
Heroes for Hire, Books 1–3
Heroes for Hire, Books 4–6
Heroes for Hire, Books 7–9
Heroes for Hire, Books 10–12
Heroes for Hire, Books 13–15

SEALs of Steel
Badger: SEALs of Steel, Book 1
Erick: SEALs of Steel, Book 2
Cade: SEALs of Steel, Book 3
Talon: SEALs of Steel, Book 4
Laszlo: SEALs of Steel, Book 5
Geir: SEALs of Steel, Book 6
Jager: SEALs of Steel, Book 7
The Final Reveal: SEALs of Steel, Book 8

SEALs of Steel, Books 1–4
SEALs of Steel, Books 5–8
SEALs of Steel, Books 1–8

The Mavericks
Kerrick, Book 1
Griffin, Book 2
Jax, Book 3
Beau, Book 4
Asher, Book 5
Ryker, Book 6
Miles, Book 7
Nico, Book 8
Keane, Book 9
Lennox, Book 10
Gavin, Book 11
Shane, Book 12

Bullard's Battle Series
Ryland's Reach, Book 1
Cain's Cross, Book 2
Eton's Escape, Book 3
Garret's Gambit, Book 4
Kano's Keep, Book 5
Fallon's Flaw, Book 6
Quinn's Quest, Book 7
Bullard's Beauty, Book 8

Collections
Dare to Be You...
Dare to Love...
Dare to be Strong...

RomanceX3

Standalone Novellas
It's a Dog's Life
Riana's Revenge
Second Chances

Published Young Adult Books:

Family Blood Ties Series
Vampire in Denial
Vampire in Distress
Vampire in Design
Vampire in Deceit
Vampire in Defiance
Vampire in Conflict
Vampire in Chaos
Vampire in Crisis
Vampire in Control
Vampire in Charge
Family Blood Ties Set 1–3
Family Blood Ties Set 1–5
Family Blood Ties Set 4–6
Family Blood Ties Set 7–9
Sian's Solution, A Family Blood Ties Series Prequel
    Novelette

Design series
Dangerous Designs
Deadly Designs
Darkest Designs
Design Series Trilogy

Standalone
In Cassie's Corner
Gem Stone (a Gemma Stone Mystery)
Time Thieves

Published Non-Fiction Books:

Career Essentials
Career Essentials: The Résumé
Career Essentials: The Cover Letter
Career Essentials: The Interview
Career Essentials: 3 in 1